A King Product

The Beginning Of The End

A Novel

JOY DEJA KING

This novel is a work of fiction. Any references to real people, events, establishments, or locales are intended only to give the fiction a sense of reality and authenticity. Other names, characters, and incidents occurring in the work are either the product of the author's imagination or are used fictitiously, as those fictionalized events and incidents that involve real persons. Any character that happens to share the name of a person who is an acquaintance of the author, past or present, is purely coincidental and is in no way intended to be an actual account involving that person.

ISBN 13: 978-1942217169
ISBN 10: 1942217161
Cover concept by Joy Deja King
Editor: Jacqueline Ruiz: tinx518@aol.com

Library of Congress Cataloging-in-Publication Data;
A King Production, King, Deja Joy
Bitch The Beginning Of The End: a series/by Joy Deja King
For complete Library of Congress Copyright info visit;
www.joydejaking.com Twitter: @joydejaking

A King Production
P.O. Box 912, Collierville, TN 38027

This Book is Dedicated To My:

Family, Readers and Supporters.
I LOVE you guys so much. Please believe that!!

A KING PRODUCTION

Who Will Live...

Who Will Die...

Bitch

The Beginning Of The End

JOY DEJA KING

Money Dies.... Love Lies... But I'll Forever Be A
Bad Bitch...

Aaliyah Carter Mills

Chapter One

Hostage

Aaliyah's finger remained steady on the trigger as she still debated whether or not to blow Maya's brains out. But as the steel metal pressed harder against the back of her own skull, she realized this wasn't the way for her to win this battle. Plus, Aaliyah was more interested in winning the war. As reality sunk in, that in her current predicament the cards were stacked against her, Aaliyah slowly lowered her gun. It was to kill but also be killed and that wasn't even an option for Aaliyah.

"Wise decision," the man with the gun pointed to the back of Aaliayah's head said.

"You really are the niece from hell," Maya snapped, yanking the gun out of Aaliyah's hand. "If we weren't related, I would've killed you by now. Move yo' lil' meddlesome ass in there!" Maya continued, leading Aaliyah to one of the bedrooms.

"Maya, you keep that gun on her while I go get some things to tie her up."

"My pleasure." Maya smiled.

"You such a dirty, lowdown bitch," Aaliyah said, shaking her head. "There is no fuckin' way we have the same blood running through our veins. I'm convinced we need a DNA test."

"It's already been done. Your dear mother insisted on it and Quentin is the father." Maya beamed as if announcing the results on the Maury Povich Show.

Aaliyah simply rolled her eyes and began cussing herself out. *Why the fuck didn't I listen to my mom and Amir. Both of them warned me to fall back and wait, but I had to jump out the window and try to kill Maya today. Now look at me. This heifa done took my gun and got it pointed at my head. Now I'm a hostage. How in the hell am I gonna get out of this shit. I was so busy trying to murder Maya's ass on the low, that don't nobody even know I'm here. This is not a good fuckin' look,* Aaliyah thought to herself letting out a deep sigh.

"I see you found everything you need," Maya commented as the man came back into the room, with rope and duct tape.

"Sure did."

Aaliyah stared at the man with the reddish brown tone and low haircut intently trying to see if she recognized his face, but got nothing. He appeared to be mixed with Cuban or something and wondered was he a part of a rival drug cartel. Then it instantly clicked for Aaliyah.

"You must be Arnez Douglass." Aaliyah frowned.

"I'm flattered. The one and only Aaliyah Carter Mills knows who I am." Arnez grinned as he tied Aaliyah's wrists and ankles to each bedpost.

Aaliyah had a million things she wanted to say to Arnez, but since none of them were nice she decided to keep them to herself. Her gut told her that he preferred if she stayed alive because he would need her for whatever plan he and Maya had devised. But at the same time, if Arnez was anything like the reputation that followed him, Aaliyah knew that he might fuck around and kill her ass if she pushed him too far. She wasn't up to taking those chances.

"You know we're not going to be able to keep her here for long. Once her family is aware she's missing, one of the first places they'll come looking is here," Maya said to Arnez.

"I know. I just wanna wait for the sun to go down and it's dark outside. Then we'll take her to the spot," Arnez replied as he finished tying up Aaliyah.

"From what I heard, you're a smart man, Arnez. So I have to wonder what made you align yourself with such a loser like Maya," Aaliyah remarked. She was trying to get a read on the mysterious man she had heard so much about, in order to get a better understanding on exactly how to deal with him.

"Shut the fuck up!" Maya barked. She wanted to shut down the conversation before it even had an opportunity to start.

"I'm not smart, I'm extremely smart. Probably one of the smartest men you'll ever have the pleasure of meeting. I'm so smart, that a supposedly dead man was able to cause more havoc to your family than anybody else ever has. That wouldn't have been possible without the assistance of Maya." Arnez glanced over at Maya and winked.

"We do make the perfect team." Maya smiled.

"Yeah, dumb and dumber," Aaliyah mumbled.

"What the fuck did you say?" Maya shot an evil glare at Aaliyah.

"I said you're playing him." Arnez tied the rope a little tighter while looking up at Aaliyah then over at Maya. "You do know she's playing you right?" Aaliyah said not letting up.

"I've had enough of you!" Maya yelled, grabbing the duct tape from the bed. She ripped off a piece. "This will shut you up." Maya jammed the tape over Aaliyah's mouth as if she wanted to smother her.

"That's enough, Maya," Arnez said without looking in her direction. "We're done here," he then said after rechecking to make sure Aaliyah was securely tied up.

"Try to stay out of trouble." Maya smirked, right behind Arnez as they headed towards the door.

"Oh and by the way, Aaliyah." Arnez paused at the doorway entrance and waited for her to lock eyes with him. "Nobody ever plays me," Arnez said it with so much certainty Aaliyah almost believed him.

Chapter Two

Going Home

As Precious descended down the stairs of the private jet, the only person on her mind was Supreme. It was as if she had awakened from her coma for the first time and the last several months had been erased. She no longer remembered being in love with Nico, her heart was with Supreme and Precious wanted her husband back.

"Mr. Carter, will I be taking you to the New Jersey estate?" the driver asked Nico once he and

Precious were settled in the awaiting car.

"No. You'll be taking my wi..." Nico stopped himself before getting the word wife out. "I mean, you'll be taking Precious to her apartment on Central Park."

"As you wish, sir." The driver nodded his head.

Nico sat back in his seat as if a heavy load was weighing him down. There was no disguising the pain that had been placed upon him. It had seeped through every inch of his body and the despair in his eyes reflected it the most.

"I'm sure the word sorry means nothing to you right now, but what more can I say. I can't make myself feel something that isn't there," Precious tried to explain.

"When we walked down that aisle and exchanged vows, I didn't think I could ever be that happy again. Then I imagined us spending the rest of our lives together and the idea of that brought me even more joy. Of course you would have to fuck it up because that would be too much like right... wouldn't it, Precious."

Precious' eyes widened in disbelief. "You're blaming me for this? Do you think I wanted things to turn out this way? My life has been turned upside down. I wake up to one man believing I'm still married to another. Then I find out I'm married to you and we're on our honeymoon. This shit is crazy to me." She sighed, shaking her head; still processing what was going on.

"Is that really so bad?"

"Is what so bad?" Precious asked, confused by Nico's question.

"Us being married."

"I'm not in love with you, Nico. I'm in love with Supreme."

"Keep telling yourself that."

"And what is that supposed to mean?"

"It means that I know you suffered some brain trauma when you were shot, but this unpredictable behavior is typical Precious Cummings. You've been going back and forth about your feelings for me and Supreme for years. Then let's not forget you had to throw Lorenzo into the love triangle. Or have you conveniently not gotten your memory back regarding that relationship? Let me get you up to speed. That was the final straw for Supreme and the reason he divorced you. He could barely tolerate knowing you still had feelings for me, but bringing another man in the mix was a game ender for him."

"You sonofabitch. I understand you're hurt and you blame me for causing your pain, but you're hitting way below the belt."

"Isn't that what we do, Precious. Continue to

hit each other below the belt," Nico stated, leaning forward. "You think it was by accident that when you almost died and woke up from that coma I was the person you remembered? I was the man you were in love with. There was a reason for that. We've had to travel different paths in our lives, but they all lead back to us because we're meant to be together. I know that and deep down in your heart you do too. But being the stubborn, irrational woman you are, who can't get through the week without having some sort of chaos in your life, you refuse to let us be happy. You know what, in spite of all that, I still want to spend the rest of my life with you. Maybe that makes me the crazy one," Nico reasoned.

"We're here, Mr. Carter," the driver said as the eerie silence between Nico and Precious seemed to be slowly suffocating everyone in the car.

"I'll have my attorney get in touch with you," Precious said removing her wedding ring from her finger and placing it in the palm of Nico's hand.

After the driver opened the back door and Precious stepped out the car, she waited for him to retrieve her luggage as the concierge from her building came out to assist him. This empty feeling swept through her that almost reminded her of death. Then Precious saw the back window roll down and although she wanted to turn away, she couldn't. For a few seconds Nico simply stared at her and Precious stared back, neither speaking a word. Before she was about to walk away, the sound of Nico's voice made her stay.

"You're my one true love and one day you'll realize that I'm yours."

Nico rolled his window back up and Precious watched as the car drove away. She realized that feeling of death that seemed to have swept through her was actually regret.

"Where to, Mr. Carter?"

"Take me to Jersey. I'm going home," Nico stated, staring out the window to get one last glimpse of Precious. He knew it might be last time he would ever see her again as his wife.

Chapter Three

M. I. H.

Amir woke up and turned over to see Latreese lying next to him, but Aaliyah was the only woman on his mind. He reached for his phone, but there weren't any calls or texts from her. After their conversation yesterday, Amir was hoping that she would've called, but then he remembered Aaliyah mentioning her mom and dad had cut their honeymoon short and were headed home.

"Good morning, baby." Latreese smiled, moving her hair out of her face.

"Sorry, did I wake you?" Amir asked, putting his phone back down on the nightstand.

"No, but I was hoping you would. I assumed I would open my eyes with you inside of me. Not you standing up with your phone." Latreese let the sheet slide down her waist exposing her breasts. Her hardened nipples let Amir know exactly where she wanted his mouth to be.

"You even wake up sexy." He grinned.

"As many times as you've woken up next to me, you should already know that," Latreese teased, giving her best bedroom eyes.

Latreese was a beautiful and sexy woman, but Amir couldn't bring himself to get back in bed with her. He regretted even allowing her to spend the night. But he was hoping she would be able to take his mind off the one person he didn't want to think about... Aaliyah. It didn't work. Having Latreese next to him only intensified his desire to be with Aaliyah and it pissed him off.

"Baby, you know I can't resist you, but I really need to go. My dad sent me a text saying he needed to see me ASAP," Amir lied.

"Come on, I'm sure you can squeeze a little time in for me." Latreese began crawling towards Amir, like a tiger on the prowl. Her tousled hair covered half her face as her hips swayed with seduction.

"Sorry, babe. I can't."

"What the fuck is going on with you, Amir? You didn't touch me last night and now you're rushing off like I have some sort of contagious disease. Normally you can't keep your hands off of me."

"I have a lot on my mind."

"Like what?" Latreese folded her arms and raised her eyebrow as if demanding to know the answer to her question.

"Business. There's a lot of turmoil going on and the shit has me stressed." That part was true, but it wasn't the reason Amir had no interest in Latreese. "Just be patient with me. I told you when we first met that my life is complicated."

"I get that, but something seems different this time."

"It's not. I'll make it up to you," Amir said giving Latreese a quick kiss on the lips before disappearing in the bathroom.

Latreese continued to sit on the bed with her arms folded in deep thought. She was well aware that her man wasn't living the typical 9 to 5 type life. She also knew that with all the stress that came with his profession, it never interfered with their sex life. There was something else going on and she planned on paying close attention to what was going on with Amir. Latreese had schemed too hard to lock down a man that could give her the lavish lifestyle she craved and she wasn't going to let anything or anybody mess it up.

Maya had fallen asleep on the couch in the living room and the last thing she remembered was her conversation with Arnez. He was about to move Aaliyah to another location, but there was some unexpected ruckus outside with some people that lived next door, so he had to wait for it to cool down. The last thing they needed was some nosey neighbor witnessing or inquiring about what Arnez was moving in the middle of the night.

Maya assumed Arnez must've come back after she fell asleep and got Aaliyah. So when she walked past the bedroom and saw her niece still tied up to the bedpost she literally freaked out.

"What the fuck are you still doing here!" Maya screamed as if Aaliyah could answer her back, which was impossible since she had duct tape covering her mouth.

Aaliyah just gave her a whatever bitch glare

and Maya rushed off to find out what was going on with Arnez. She ran to her bedroom to retrieve her burner phone and called Arnez. He finally picked up on the fourth ring.

"Where the hell are you?! And why is Aaliyah still tied up in my apartment?" she yelled.

"Calm the fuck down. I'll be over there shortly."

"Are you crazy! If they don't know by now, soon her family is going to know Aaliyah is missing and they are going to make a beeline straight to me. I can't have her in this apartment. Everything will be ruined!"

"Like I said, I'll be there shortly. Relax. We still have time. She'll be gone before they get there. Now let me finish what I need to do so I can get over there," Arnez said and ended the call.

"I should've known better than partnering up with that psycho!" Maya hollered at her phone before tossing it on the bed. She began pacing back and forth in her room. "Well at least Nico and Precious are on their honeymoon. That should buy me a little bit of time," Maya said, talking to herself out loud. "But I can't afford to take any chances. Arnez needs to hurry up because if they find Aaliyah here my life is over."

When Amir finally made it out of his apartment and away from Latreese, the first thing he did was call Aaliyah. Her phone went straight to voicemail and that didn't sit well with him. With the new information they discussed regarding Maya and Arnez, Amir figured Aaliyah would have her phone glued to her ear, waiting for any updates. He tried calling her again, but got the same results. He decided to head to her mom's apartment since she had been staying there.

"Good afternoon," the doorman said to Amir when he walked into the building.

"Hey, Pedro. How are things going for you today?" Amir asked, making small talk.

"You know, the regular," Pedro replied with the same standard pleasant smile he seemed to keep plastered across his face.

"As long as you good, then that's all that matters."

"Of course, sir, and yes, I am good."

"Glad to hear. So have you seen Aaliyah today?" Amir questioned ready to move past the polite chatter.

"No, I haven't. I saw Mrs. Carter last night, but not Aaliyah. I just got here about an hour ago so maybe she came this morning."

"Okay, well can you call and let them know I'm on my way up."

"Of course."

Amir waited for Pedro to make the call and once he acknowledged it was okay to go up, he got on the elevator. He didn't ask who he spoke to, but Amir was optimistic that Aaliyah would be the one greeting him. He pressed the doorbell and within a minute the door opened.

"I'm sure you were expecting my daughter to answer." Precious smiled. "How are you, Amir? Come in."

"I'm good. How about you? How was your honeymoon?" With the awkward silence that followed after his question, Amir immediately hated he even asked. "So is Aaliyah in her bedroom?" Amir questioned, trying to change the subject.

"Actually Aaliyah isn't here. That was one of the reasons I wanted you to come up. I was hoping you could tell me where she might be. I've been calling her since last night and I can't get her on the phone. Now it's going straight to voicemail. Did she mention she might be going out of town or anything?" Precious asked.

"No, she didn't. I've been trying to call her too. That's why I came over because I couldn't reach her and I was a little worried," Amir admitted.

"Worried... is Aaliyah in some sort of trouble?"

"She came to see me yesterday and we talked about some things."

"Things like what?" Precious could tell that Amir was hesitating. "This isn't the time to hold back, Amir. If something is going on with my daughter you need to speak up... now!"

"I mentioned to her some things I found out about this man Arnez and his possible involvement with Maya," Amir revealed.

"Maya?"

"Yes. But I told her that I spoke with my dad and he was going to handle it. I told her he wanted us to stay out of it, but you know Aaliyah...." Amir put his head down, trying to conceal how concerned he was.

Precious began thinking about what Amir said and then the last conversation she had with Aaliyah seemed to pop in her head out of nowhere. Her memories of certain incidents and conversations were still so sketchy. Some things flowed effortlessly and others she had to somewhat piece together.

"Before I left for my honeymoon, Aaliyah did mention finding out some questionable things about Maya. I told her to wait before acting on it, at least until I got back from our trip. She promised she would but knowing how Aaliyah feels about that trifling Maya, I doubt she kept that promise."

"I thought you and Maya were becoming close?" Amir questioned, surprised at the negative tone Precious had towards her.

"That was before my memory came back... or at least some more of it. I can't believe I actually had a soft spot for that devilish sister of mine."

"None of us could," Amir conceded.

"Well, blame that bullet I took. Now come on let's go," Precious said grabbing her purse.

"Where are we going?"

"To Maya's apartment. On a positive note, when the three of us was one little happy family Quentin gave me a key to her apartment. He wanted me to have it in case there was ever any sort of emergency and I needed to get inside. I would call this an emergency."

"I would have to agree. But do you think Maya could've really hurt Aaliyah?"

"Maya is a very sick and demented woman. I don't put anything past her. The only reason she might not hurt Aaliyah is because she knows her obituary is already written if she does. But I've learned the hard way to never underestimate Maya, especially if her back is pushed against the wall. Now let's go! I have to find my daughter."

Chapter Four

Close Call

With the chaos Maya had already been through and her day wasn't even over, she welcomed the hot water drenching over her body. She was completely immersed in her shower and welcomed a moment of silence to gather her thoughts. So when she stepped out the bathroom and was greeted with Precious and Amir staring down her throat, her heart dropped.

"Precious, what are you doing here," Maya

stuttered.

"Why so nervous, Maya? Your hand is shaking so bad, if you don't be careful you might drop your towel. I'm sure you don't want to show us your naked body or do you?" Precious hissed.

"Of course I'm nervous. You scared me. How did you get in here anyway?" Maya questioned, holding her towel tighter against her body.

"Our father gave me a copy. He wanted your big sister to have it in case an emergency came up. I did knock and when you didn't answer I got worried."

"I'm fine so you and Amir can go now."

"Why are you rushing us off? Aren't you going to invite us to sit down, maybe have some milk and cookies?" Precious said with sarcasm.

"Aren't you supposed to be on your honeymoon?" Maya continued to fiddle with her towel as her eyes darted around.

"It got cut short. I'm trying to locate my daughter. Would you have any idea where Aaliyah might be?"

"Why would I know where Aaliyah is?"

"Why do you sound defensive?" Precious stepped closer towards Maya. So close that she could smell the scent of the fresh toothpaste on Maya's breath.

"And why do you keep glancing over at the

door?" Amir asked. Stepping out of his role as silent observer. Amir didn't wait for Maya to answer. Instead he headed in that direction.

"Don't go in there!" Maya yelled with panic in her voice. She tried to walk past Precious and catch up with Amir.

Precious yanked Maya's arm with quickness. Her pull was so intense for a second Maya thought she had dislocated her shoulder.

"Ouch! That hurt!" Maya belted, using her other arm to rub her shoulder that was in pain.

"That was the point." Precious frowned, letting go of Maya's arm then shoving her out the way. By the time Precious got to the room, Amir had already opened the door. "Did you find anything?"

"No." Amir stood in the middle of the room with his hands in his pocket looking around.

"I don't know what you expected to find in here, but I would appreciate if both of you would leave."

"I don't know what is going on, but something is up with you. You're standing there trying to appear calm, but the fear in your eyes is telling me something different. What are you so afraid of, Maya?" Precious pressed her for an answer, but Maya wasn't saying a thing.

"You barge in my home. Attack me when I

get out the shower. Of course I seem afraid! I'm not feeling well and all I wanted to do was relax and take an afternoon nap. Last time I checked that wasn't a crime."

Precious seemed to be staring right through Maya and she wondered if her sister could see the beads of sweat building on her forehead.

"Any signs that Aaliyah has been here?" Precious questioned taking her attention off Maya and talking to Amir.

"Nothing yet," Amir answered now standing in front of the window.

Maya watched nervously as Amir continued to look around. She tried to keep her cool as she moved closer to a table next to the bed. When Arnez was untying Aaliyah, a bracelet she was wearing came off and fell on the bed. Maya hadn't noticed until they had already left. She put it on the small table next to the bed and the only thing blocking it was a lamp. Maya planned on getting rid of the bracelet thinking she had a little bit of time. Never did she anticipate Precious and Amir showing up inside of her apartment and catching her off guard.

"Like I told you, no one is here. I haven't spoken to Aaliyah and I have no idea where she is. Maybe she decided to take a trip with that cute boyfriend of hers. What's his name again, Amir..."

Maya said trying to get under his skin.

"I don't see anything here, Precious," Amir said, ignoring Maya's question.

"Well, let's look around some more before we leave," Precious said, rolling her eyes at Maya.

"Be my guest," Maya said graciously. Relieved the duo was exiting the room she had Aaliyah stashed in, Maya was confident that there was no other trace of her being there. The moment she heard them walking down the hall, Maya retrieved the bracelet and buried it under the mattress. She casually walked back out into the hallway and headed to the kitchen.

Precious and Amir spent the next twenty minutes dissecting every inch of Maya's apartment. The place wasn't that big, but they were looking for any clue that Aaliyah had been there.

"I'm not finding anything," Amir huffed. "Doesn't look like Aaliyah was ever here."

"Yeah, I'm not finding anything either. I don't know whether to be disappointed or relieved," Precious said to Amir as they walked towards the living room.

"It's a little uncomfortable walking around in this towel. Are you all finished so I can relax and take a nap," Maya sniped, coming out the kitchen.

"Yes, we're done here... for now." It was obvious from her tone that Precious wasn't done with Maya and she knew it.

"We're sisters. What happened? I thought we were becoming close. Just a few weeks ago we were having dinner with our father, now you're treating me like I'm your enemy." The sorrow in Maya's voice almost sounded genuine.

"That's because you are the enemy," Precious spit, slamming Maya against the wall. "You listen to me you no good piece of shit." Precious had her hand firmly gripped around Maya's throat as the water from her wet hair dripped down her neck. "You better not be lying to me. If I find out you know where my daughter is, dear old dad won't be able to save yo' ass this time. Now we can go, Amir," Precious said letting Maya go.

"I would never hurt Aaliyah. She's my niece." Maya coughed, leaning over trying to regain her composure. "We're family. You need to remember that," Maya belted between coughs as she watched Precious and Amir walk out the front door.

"So what do you think?" Amir questioned as he and Precious got in the car.

"With Maya there's no telling. How 'bout you?"

"I hate to say it, but Maya might be right.

Aaliyah could've taken off with Dale or she might've gone away by herself for a few days. She has done it before."

"That's true. Although I don't like using the word right and Maya in the same sentence, for this particular situation I do hope Maya is right. I'm not taking any chances though. We need to keep at least two men on her at all times until we find out what is going on," Precious said looking out the rearview mirror before switching lanes.

"I agree."

"I'm leaving for LA tonight, but I'll only be gone for a day, two max. Hopefully one of us will hear from Aaliyah by the time I get back. If not..." Precious paused.

"If not what?" Amir asked, wanting Precious to finish her sentence.

Precious came to a stop at the red light and turned towards Amir. "If not... then we'll wreck havoc through every city until we find Aaliyah, starting with New York."

Chapter Five

I Won't Give Up On Us

"How long do you plan on keeping me locked up in this place?" Aaliyah wanted to know. "I mean these accommodations aren't exactly five star."

"You shouldn't be complaining. You were able to shower. I fed you and gave you clean clothes to put on. The best part is you're no longer tied up with duct tape over your mouth."

"Aren't you the perfect gentleman, Arnez. Thank you because I'm not worthy of your hospitality and generosity," Aaliyah said full of cynicism.

"I understand you might feel this place is beneath you, growing up in mansions with unlimited access to money and all, but you'll have to deal."

"Yeah, but for how long?" She folded her arms, leaning back on a dingy brown couch. Aaliyah shook her head as she looked around what looked like a basement apartment. It had a tiny bathroom and an even tinier kitchen.

"I haven't decided yet." Arnez shrugged, reading a text message on his phone.

"How long are you going to keep me alive before you kill me?" Aaliyah's question was so blunt and unexpected that Arnez immediately stopped reading the text that had his undivided attention and focused on her.

"Who said I planned on killing you?"

"I've seen your face. If you let me live, you know my family will come at you with a vengeance. So it's not if you're going to kill me, but when."

"Amir has already informed his father that I'm alive. So Genesis will be coming after me with a vengeance anyway." Arnez smiled.

"How do you know that?"

Arnez was amused by the puzzled look on Aaliyah's face. "I've managed to stay alive a very long time for a man that's supposed to be dead. That means I'm far from stupid and I'm able to figure most things out before they actually happen."

"Does that mean you knew I was going to show up at Maya's place to kill her?"

"Nope. That caught me off guard. That's why I have no idea how long I plan on keeping you here. This is a real inconvenience for me."

"You can always let me go."

"You've become an added bonus. Now I have to figure out how to use you to my advantage. Once I do, then I'll be able to answer your question. Until then, try not to give me any problems. Excuse me, I have a phone call to make."

Aaliyah watched as Arnez disappeared into the bedroom. It was literally a few steps away, but there was a door and he closed it.

"Maya, I need you to get over here and look after Aaliyah. I have some important shit to handle," Arnez informed her.

"I can't."

"What you mean you can't?"

"Precious and Amir showed up at my apartment unexpectedly. I was in the shower. Precious had a key that our father gave her. If they had come any earlier, they would've caught you taking Aaliyah out of here."

"But they didn't. So get yo' ass over here so I can go handle my business."

"I can't!" Maya screamed. Did you not hear what I said? Precious came over here looking for Aaliyah. They're worried about her and they thought I had something to do with her disappearance."

"Really... so soon? I thought you said Precious was on her honeymoon and that you all were cool."

"She got some of her memory back and remembers hating my guts." Maya sighed. "Trust me, they have someone watching my apartment and are monitoring every move I make. I can't go anywhere near Aaliyah. When I saw you calling me, I went outside in the hallway. I'm afraid to even talk in my own crib."

"Well you need to figure some shit out. I would just leave her here, but I can tell Aaliyah is not only sneaky, but also resourceful. She might figure a way out of this place. I wanna go through it thoroughly before I leave her here alone and I don't have time for all that right now. I need to go," Arnez said.

"So what do you expect for me to do?"

"Get a fuckin' babysitter over here... ASAP!

That's what the fuck I expect for you to do."

"Fine! I think I have somebody that I can trust to do it. But you need to figure out a way to get Precious off my back," Maya responded.

"You let me handle that. Just have yo' people here within an hour." Before Maya could respond, Arnez had already hung up.

While Arnez was on the phone, Aaliyah had quickly gotten up trying to see if there was any opportunity for her to make a getaway. But as raggedy as the place was it was locked down and secure like Fort Knox. There was one entrance and exit, with bars and boards plus two locks.

"Damn, ain't nobody gettin' out this motherfucker," Aaliyah huffed. She went over to the kitchen to see if there were any knives, forks, anything lying around that could be used as a weapon but she came up empty.

"I've should've known you were out here schemin'," Arnez grumbled.

"No, I was just checking to see if you had any water. I was thirsty."

"Save it. This is exactly why I'm not leaving you here alone."

"Please, there's no escaping this place," Aaliyah said, putting her hands inside the gray hoodie Arnez gave her to put on.

"If you were anybody else I might believe

that but you… I'm not taking any chances."

"I have to give you credit for not underestimating me."

"I know who your mother and father are. To underestimate you would make me a stupid man and we've both established that's something I'm not."

"Seeing who you've partnered up with, I'm still not convinced. Maya is a loose cannon. It's only a matter of time before she crosses you. Don't say I didn't warn you, Arnez," Aaliyah said, turning on the television.

It had been a few minutes since Maya got off the phone with Arnez. She was torn about what to do next. Maya continued pacing the hallway debating whether or not to place a certain phone call. Her options were limited and under the circumstances she didn't have much of a choice.

"Fuck it!" she said before making the call. Even as the phone rang, Maya was arguing with herself and was about to hang up until the person on the other end answered.

"Hey, what's up?"

"I need for you to do something for me and I need you to do it right now…" Maya said, praying she wouldn't regret her decision.

Precious arrived at Supreme's house and stood staring at the door before finally ringing the doorbell. She had butterflies in her stomach and didn't know if that was good or bad. She was excited to see her ex-husband and believed he would reciprocate those feelings.

"Can I help you?" a woman wearing cut off jeans shorts and a cropped baby blue t-shirt opened the door and asked. She looked too old to be a friend of Xavier, but too young to be dealing with Supreme.

"Who are you?" Precious questioned, stepping forward.

"You're at my door, so I think I should be asking you that question." The woman had a smile on her face, but her tone screamed who the fuck are you.

"I must have the wrong house because I'm looking for someone named Supreme."

"No, you have the right house." The woman then leaned against the door and squinted her eyes with an attitude as if trying to figure out who the woman was standing in front of her.

"Great! Then you can step aside so I can see Supreme and my son," Precious said now moving from the front step to the door entrance, but the woman was using her body to block her pathway. "Are you going to move or do I have to move you?"

"Who's at the door, Morgan?" Supreme walked up asking before she had a chance to respond to Precious. "Precious, what are you doing here?" he questioned, visibly surprised to see her.

"I came to see you and Xavier."

"Well come in." Supreme reached out his hand as Morgan moved out the way, allowing Precious to get past her.

"How have you been? How's Xavier?"

"Xavier's good. He should be home shortly. I apologize, Precious this is Morgan. Morgan this is Xavier's mother and my ex-wife, Precious," Supreme said, introducing the women.

"Nice to meet you, Precious," Morgan said in a chipper sweet voice. In contrast to the not so welcoming tone she greeted Precious with. Precious didn't even bother pretending she had any interest in Morgan. She kept her attention on Supreme.

"Supreme, can we talk in private?"

"Sure. Let's go into my office. Morgan, I'll be back."

"No problem." Morgan grinned as if she didn't have a care in the world. Precious gave the woman a quick glance before following Supreme in his office. She reminded her of Nia Long, back when she played in Boyz In The Hood. Pretty girl, but way too young to be playing house with Supreme, at least in Precious' opinion.

"So what brings you all the way to LA? Last I heard you were on your honeymoon," Supreme said, taking a seat behind his desk. Precious sat down on the couch across from him and gazed at Supreme for a moment. His chiseled face and smooth brown skin hadn't aged at all. He looked exactly the same as the day Precious met him at the celebrity car show so many years ago. "Are you okay?" Supreme stood up and questioned. "Your mind seems to be someplace else."

"I apologize." Precious then paused as if getting her thoughts together, and looked around Supreme's office which was hand constructed of oak, mahogany, and redwood. "These last few days I have had a lot on my mind. A lot of it has to do with you."

"With me? Let me guess. You're feeling guilty for not remembering being married to me and running off with the love of your life, Nico. Like I told you before, I forgive you. You took a bullet for me and in the process you forgot ever loving me. How can I be mad at you for that," Supreme said, sitting back down.

"The thing is I do remember."

"Remember what?"

"Us, our love. How much…"

"Stop." Supreme raised his hand and shook his head. "Don't do it."

"Don't do what? Don't you want to hear what I have to say?" Precious asked, rushing towards Supreme.

"No, I don't. I can't do this with you, Precious. I don't wanna do it," Supreme stated, turning away.

"I know I've hurt you so many times and you've hurt me, too. But I know in my heart we love each other and we belong together."

"What does your husband have to say about this? I doubt Nico agrees with you." Precious was silent and Supreme could see the distress in her eyes. "Please don't tell me all these memories came flooding back to you on your honeymoon."

"Nico is hurt right now, but I know eventually he'll understand."

"You don't even believe that." Supreme put his head down, shaking it back and forth. "Damn! I don't even like Nico, but even he doesn't deserve no shit like that."

"Do you think I wanted this to happen? My life has been turned upside down. I just want things to go back to the way they used to be."

"Well since you got your memory back, then

you know the reason we got a divorce had nothing to do with Nico, but your affair with Lorenzo. So there's no going back."

"Supreme, a love like ours doesn't die. I know when I got shot you were praying I survived so we could be together again. I know it."

"Maybe that's true. But when you woke up and didn't remember me... us, I said to myself it wasn't meant to be. It was hard for me to accept that you wanted to spend the rest of your life with Nico, but I did and I moved on."

"Moved on to what?" Precious flung up her arms. "That little teeny bopper in your living room."

"Morgan is twenty-four."

"Yeah, young enough to be besties with your daughter," Precious shot back.

"But she's not." Supreme walked over to the window that had city and ocean views. "When I stand right here and look out this window, this is where I get the most peace."

"Peace... is that what you're looking for?"

"Yes, it is and Morgan gives me that. After you, I was emotionally drained. She comes with no baggage and no expectations. That's what I need in my life."

"Supreme, you need a lot more than that to be happy. Morgan is simply a filler."

"I'm good with that. It's a lot better than that non-stop rollercoaster you kept me on."

"I'll admit, we had our ups and downs, but it was real... our love is real.

Supreme turned and faced Precious. "You're not nineteen anymore and I'm not in my twenties. I'm tired. You have to know when it's time to let go. We had our moment. We share two beautiful kids together and I'll always love you, Precious," Supreme said, stroking the side of her cheek. "But there's no going back."

Precious bit down on her bottom lip. She felt her eyes about to water up. When she heard her cell phone ringing, she welcomed the interruption.

"I need to get this," she said answering her phone. "Hello."

"Hey, mom."

"Aaliyah! Omigoodness I've been worried about you. I'm so happy you called. Where are you and why is your number coming up unknown?" Precious questioned, glancing down at her phone.

"I lost my phone so I'm calling you from the hotel I'm staying at. I guess that's how their number shows up."

"Hotel... where are you?"

"I'm in Real del Mar."

"What are you doing in Mexico?" Precious sounded puzzled.

"With everything that's been going on, I needed to get away before I did something that I would regret."

"You mean like go after Maya?"

"That's exactly what I mean."

"I'm just relieved you're safe. When are you coming back to New York?"

"Not sure yet. But I'll be in touch and let you know. I'm sorry I had you so worried. I thought you were on your honeymoon and I would be back before you."

"No problem, baby girl. I'm just so happy to hear your voice."

"I would love to talk some more, but I have some people waiting on me. I'll call you back soon."

"Make sure you do that. I love you."

"I love you too, mom."

"Is everything okay with Aaliyah?" Supreme asked when Precious got off the phone.

"Yes, I mean I think so."

"What do you mean you think?"

"She sounded fine, but something doesn't feel right, but I'm not sure what. Maybe I'm being paranoid because of my sneaky ass sister."

"What does Maya have to do with any of

this?"

"Before I left on my honeymoon with Nico, Aaliyah came to me with some concerns about Maya."

"Concerns like what?"

"She thought that Maya was involved with the shooting at the warehouse and the other crazy shit that's been happening to our family and that some man named Arnez was helping her."

"Arnez... he's dead."

"You know Arnez?"

"No," Supreme quickly stated. "I've heard of him. I don't see how a dead man could be helping Maya."

"True, but supposedly this Arnez cat isn't actually dead."

"Really... that's interesting," Supreme said walking back over to the window, rubbing his chin.

"The good news is clearly Maya doesn't have Aaliyah held up somewhere. The bad news is hearing Aaliyah's voice still didn't get rid of this knot I have in the pit of my stomach."

"Did you have any intentions of telling me you were worried about our daughter?" Supreme wanted to know.

"I didn't want to get you all riled up if I was overreacting and Aaliyah was fine which obviously she is."

"So she's in Mexico?"

"Yes."

"With who?"

"She didn't say. All she said was some people were waiting for her and she would call me back. She also lost her cell phone. That explains why she hasn't answered my calls or text messages."

"Aaliyah is my daughter too."

"I know that, Supreme."

"Sometimes I think you forget. If you ever think something has happened to her or she's in trouble you need to come to me."

"You're right and I apologize. But luckily we don't have anything to worry about. Speaking of our kids, I was thinking that maybe when school lets out, Xavier can stay with me for the summer."

"I don't know if that's a good idea," Supreme said with reluctance.

"I do. After I lost my memory I didn't even remember our son. Now that things are starting to come back to me, my first priority is rebuilding my relationship with Xavier. There was a time we were very close and I want to get that back before it's too late."

"Xavier is old enough to make that decision, but I won't try to stop him if it's what he wants too."

"Thank you. You don't mind if I wait around

until he gets home?"

"Of course not. You're his mother. No matter what has happened between us, Precious, I would never try to stop you from trying to have a relationship with our son. He needs both of us in his life."

"I remember when you used to need me too. I'm not giving up faith that one day you'll need me again."

As Supreme parted his lips to respond, Precious put her index finger over his mouth. She closed her eyes and gave him a soft kiss before walking out.

Chapter Six

My Story

"Are you satisfied!" Aaliyah sulked, flinging the phone out of her face.

"Yes. You did an excellent job... very convincing." Arnez smiled with satisfaction.

"You didn't leave me a choice. You threatened to hurt Amir if I didn't make the call. Then you had me on that stupid speaker, listening to every word my mother said." Aaliyah rolled her eyes.

"I have to be careful with you. If you're awake

you're scheming. But it's good to know you're able to follow instructions when necessary."

"Whatever, Arnez. I thought you had somewhere to be so why don't you be gone." Aaliyah shooed her hand as if sweeping Arnez away.

"I love how feisty you are, even though you know your life is in my hands."

"If you wanted me dead, I would be dead already. For whatever reason you want to keep me alive. So if I choose to talk shit then so be it." Aaliyah shrugged, taking a sip of the water Arnez gave her.

"Don't get too comfortable. I can always change my mind," Arnez commented. They then both looked up as they heard a distinct knock at the door. "That must be your babysitter."

"I wonder if that's Maya's trifling ass," Aaliyah mumbled. "I would rather be stuck with Arnez then have to look at Maya's fuckin' face," she said.

"You must be who Maya sent over," Arnez said when he opened the door.

"Yeah, I hope I got the secret knock correct. Maya told me so fast so I wasn't sure."

"Nah, you got it right."

"She didn't say what you needed me for just to get over here quick."

"Follow me," Arnez said walking back into

the room where Aaliyah was. "I need you to keep a very close eye on this young lady while I'm gone."

"What the fuck! I knew you were a lowlife, worthless piece of shit, but never did I guess you were this pathetic," Aaliyah spit when she looked up and saw Latreese standing behind Arnez.

"I take it you ladies know each other." Arnez laughed.

Latreese's mouth was still on the floor from the shock of seeing Aaliyah. "Maya didn't tell me you wanted me over here to watch Aaliyah. I... I..."

"No need to stutter," Arnez joked, finding it funny how shook Latreese seemed.

"She stuttering because she know I'ma whoop her ass the moment she's left alone with me," Aaliyah promised.

"We won't be having none of that because the cuffs are going back on," Arnez stated. "I know you didn't think I was gonna let you be free with her watching you." Arnez chuckled, pointing his fnger at Latreese.

"I can handle her." Latreese stepped forward, finally opening her mouth to speak. "Ain't nobody scared of you, Aaliyah."

"Giiiiirl," Aaliyah shook her head and laughed. "I see you conjured up some fake courage."

"I have some place to be so I can't entertain you ladies right now," Arnez said as he tied Aaliyah up. "This will keep Aaliyah out of your hair, but Latreese, don't take advantage of the situation," Arnez stated firmly.

"What does that mean?" Latreese gave Arnez a perplexing look.

"It means don't fuck wit' me just because I'm all tied up." Aaliyah was still popping shit even though all the cards seemed to be stacked against her.

"I wasn't talking to you." Latreese rolled her neck and slit her eyes at Aaliyah and set her sights on Arnez.

"I want her alive and not so much as a scratch on her. Are we clear?"

"Yes, we're clear," Latreese reluctantly agreed.

"Good, you girls try to behave until I get back."

The moment Arnez grabbed his keys and left, Aaliyah was back talking shit. "You better hope Maya kills yo' ass before Amir finds out what a snake you are, 'cause it ain't gon' be pretty."

"Shut up! How in the hell did Arnez tie you all up, but forget to tape up that mouth of yours," Latreese snapped, looking around to see if she could find something to shut Aaliyah up.

"He didn't forget. Arnez wanted me to be free to pop shit to yo' dumb ass. Tell me, how did Maya convince you to come over and play babysitter. Oh yes, she didn't tell you. Maya used you to do her dirty work."

"You don't know what you're talking about."

"Yes, I do. I saw how freaked out you looked when you noticed me sitting on this couch. You were completely blindsided. You know what, I actually owe you an apology."

"Excuse me, what did you say?" Latreese sounded confused and Aaliyah knew she would be.

"I want to apologize."

"Why?"

"Because for you to be here, Maya must have some real dirt on you. So you're a victim too."

Latreese began playing with her hair, nervously putting her head down. Aaliyah felt she was on to something so she decided to push a little more.

"I mean why else would you risk your relationship with Amir unless Maya left you no choice."

"It's no secret we aren't besties, but I had no idea you were being held hostage and Maya was behind it. I swear."

"I believe you, Latreese," Aaliyah said in her

most understanding voice without sounding too phony. "Maya can be extremely cunning and she has no problem taking advantage of people. Especially when she thinks you need her. So I have to ask, what do you need Maya for?"

Aaliyah could see Latreese was hesitant to reveal what Maya was holding over her head, but pressed on using a different approach.

"We don't have to talk about it," Aaliyah said as if she didn't care one way or the other. "You just seemed like you wanted someone to confide in, but I totally understand if you prefer that someone not be me." Aaliyah then pretended like she was watching some Lifetime movie she had turned to before Arnez tied her up.

It took twenty minutes of Aaliyah paying Latreese no mind before she finally cracked.

"Believe it or not, Maya saved my life."

"Huh? Sorry! I got so caught up watching this movie that I wasn't paying attention to what you said." Aaliyah gave her best apologetic face.

"No problem. All I said was that Maya was the one who saved my life."

"Really. How's that?" Aaliyah casually questioned then glanced back at the television as if Latreese still didn't have her full attention. All that did was make Latreese want to talk more.

"Maya paid for my freedom."

"Paid for your freedom?" Aaliyah gave Latreese a baffled stare. "Last I heard owning slaves was illegal."

"Yeah, but it goes on every day in the sex trade world."

Aaliyah didn't want Latreese to know it, but although she had been paying attention before, now she had her undivided attention. Aaliyah still played it cool though. Instead of replying to what Latreese said, she sat quietly and waited for her to reveal more.

"I'm the text book case of the girl from the hood with the hard knock life. Father in jail, mother strung out on drugs. Only difference is, when I was thirteen my mother sold me to a drug dealer/pimp named Gomez for some crack."

"Excuse me? Did I hear that correctly?"

"Yes. For the first couple years Gomez didn't pimp me out. I would cook and clean for him. I still looked young so he would use me to carry drugs and stuff like that because he thought I would never be on the cops radar. For the rough life I had been exposed to growing up, in a lot of ways I was a late bloomer. I was a virgin and I didn't start developing physically until I was about fifteen, almost sixteen. Once that happened..." Latreese's voice trailed off as she stared up at the ceiling.

"Latreese, we really don't have to talk about

this."

"No, I want to. I've never told anybody my story. I was too ashamed. I still am."

"You don't have to be ashamed. You were a kid. None of what happened to you is your fault."

"That might be true, but it doesn't change anything. I tried to hide my budding figure under big clothes for as long as I could. But one day Gomez walked in my bedroom unexpectedly and caught me taking off my clothes. That night he forced himself on me. He started having sex with me whenever he wanted for the next year or so. Then one day out the blue he said he thought I was ready to be put to work. Never in my worst nightmare did I think work meant having sex with random men. He was bad enough, but the other men." Latreese sighed, shaking her head. "It was depressing. I can't tell you how many times I contemplated ending my life."

"I can't begin to imagine how hard that had to be on you."

"There are no words to describe it. When the day came that I couldn't take it anymore, I tried to run away. I left with just the clothes on my back. It took Gomez less than a few hours to locate me. He beat me to the brink of death. He said my crackhead mother sold me and I would spend the rest of my life working for him until he decided I was no longer worth keeping around."

"What an evil man. So how did you end up meeting Maya?"

"As the years progressed, Gomez began moving up in the drug game. Maya began doing some business with him."

"Is that right." This story was becoming more and more intriguing for Aaliyah.

"Yes. Gomez had this after hours lounge in Queens. He conducted a lot of his business there. He would have his main girls there a lot, in case any of his customers wanted our services."

"So wait, Maya was getting down with the ladies?"

"No... no. She would never hire the girls for sex, it was always business with her. But maybe after the third or fourth time I saw her there, she sparked up a conversation. Asking me how old I was, if I was Gomez's girlfriend or did I work for him."

"Why did she think you were Gomez's girlfriend?"

"All pimps have their favorite girls that they keep within arms reach even though they're still selling them like a piece of meat. Gomez always kept me by his side unless a customer was offering him a price he couldn't resist."

"Got you. So wait... Maya bought you from

Gomez?"

"Yes. A couple days after Maya had that conversation with me, Gomez told me to pack my stuff up because I was leaving. At first, I didn't know what was going on. I wanted to believe he was putting me out and I would finally have my freedom, but I knew that would be too good to be true. Then I went downstairs and saw Maya standing in the living room. That's when Gomez informed me that I now belonged to Maya and I better do whatever she says because she paid a pretty penny for me."

"Why in the hell would Maya want to buy you?"

"I was asking myself the same question. Initially I figured she ran a prostitution ring and recruited me to be one of her girls."

"So wait, Maya was running hoes?"

"I figured as much, but I was wrong. She had bigger plans for me. Maya said that she thought I would clean up well and was the perfect age for something she needed me to do."

"Which was what?"

"Help her find out what was going on within an organization by seducing the son of one of its members."

"Amir," Aaliyah blurted out.

"Yes. I went from being Kendra Watkins to

Latreese Lawson. Maya gave me a whole new identity. She registered me for school. Put me in an apartment. Bought me all new clothes and once she thought I was ready, she made sure I was dangled in front of Amir like an irresistible piece of candy and he did bite."

"I have to give it to Maya, she came up with a perfect plan."

"Except she never counted on a damaged girl like me falling in love with her mark, but I did."

"Latreese, this is not gonna end well for you. Trust me, I know Maya. She's a user... the worst kind. Once she's done getting everything she needs from you, she will kill you. If there's any chance of you getting out of this alive, you better come clean with Amir and cut your losses. Or Maya won't be the only person you'll need to watch your back for," Aaliyah warned.

Chapter Seven

Ties That Bind Us

Arnez pulled up to the isolated warehouse in Staten Island by the pier. The cool breeze coming from the water made it feel more like a brisk fall day and almost made Arnez forget they were nearing the end of spring. He hurried inside not wanting to keep the man he was meeting waiting.

"My man, Arnez. I'm glad you were able to meet up with me on such short notice."

"You said it was important and when it comes

to business I ain't no slacker." Arnez smirked.

"No doubt."

"Talk to me. Tell me what has the usually calm, cool, and collected Emory all worked up," Arnez inquired.

"I wanted you to know, I informed Aaliyah that you were alive. She was becoming increasingly suspicious of me and planting all sorts of negative seeds in my brother's ear. I had to get her off my back and try to gain a little bit of her trust. What better way then to feed her some information that I knew she would find extremely helpful."

"I get it. Doesn't really matter since Amir's people had already dug that information up."

"Exactly. So me telling her something that she already knew, but thought was a secret made what I said even more credible. I think I played my cards very well."

"I agree. So what do you think Aaliyah's next move will be?" Arnez questioned wanting to see if Emory had any idea Aaliyah was now on the missing persons list.

"Of course I'm sure she ran off to tell her family. But what can they do? They stay losing, we always a step ahead. By the time they figure all this shit out, their entire operation will be out of commission. Hopefully by then Dale will be done wit' Aaliyah's ass and she'll be out of commission with the rest of her family."

"You sound like you got this all figured out." Arnez was amused.

"Man, that broad is such a nightmare. She been giving me a headache from day one. She's the typical privileged brat that swears the world revolves around her ass. Little does Aaliyah know we the real puppet masters and we lettin' her play in our world," Emory boasted.

"Very true. Maybe we need to go ahead and eliminate Aaliyah now," Arnez suggested.

"Nah. That would raise way too much suspicion. Dale would be all up my ass and everybody else's trying to figure out who was responsible for that shit. We need to keep Aaliyah alive and well. If and when Dale veto her out, then we'll decide what to do with her if she's a problem."

"Understood. Our plan is coming together even better than I thought it would. No need in rocking the boat."

Emory nodded his head in agreement. "You're a very smart man, Arnez. I knew we would make great partners."

"I miss you already," Skylar said kissing Genesis on his lips, before getting back to putting her clothes in the suitcase. "Luckily when I come back I'll be with my son and we'll be living in New York, close to you," Skylar beamed. "Have you decided on the realtor you want to use yet? I know the last time we talked about it, you had narrowed it down to two."

"I actually did make a decision."

"Great! We'll be back in a week so I'll be ready. I can't wait to see the different options." Skylar smiled, folding up her last pair of jeans.

Genesis sat down on the edge of the bed and put his head down. "Listen..."

"Babe, can you pass me those shoes," Skylar said, cutting Genesis off. He handed her the shoes and Skylar put them in the suitcase oblivious to Genesis' mood shift.

Genesis put his hand on top of Skylar's to pause her packing. "Skylar, why don't you sit down?"

"Sure. But babe if you're going to ask me to stay for a few more days I really need to get back home. I have a ton of stuff to get done so this move can go smoothly. But I'll be back soon.

Don't worry, I hate leaving you too," Skylar said reaching over to kiss Genesis again.

"I've decided it's not a good idea for you and your son to move here."

Genesis' words stung Skylar to the core. She was speechless and motionless. She then went back to packing her clothes as if she didn't hear a word Genesis said. Skylar was trying her best to delete the last sentence out of his mouth from history.

"Skylar, I know you're disappointed, but it's for the best."

"The best for who? Certainly not me." Skylar was now forcibly tossing the last of her belongings in the suitcase as if taking her frustrations out on her stuff.

"My organization is in the midst of a war and I'm not even sure who we're fighting. I have an idea, but nothing has been solidified."

"And? That should make you want me to be closer to you more than ever."

"Why would I want that? So you can be another innocent causality in my bullshit. You know how many loved ones I've lost in my line of business. If something happened to you or, God forbid, your son because of me…" Genesis' words became inaudible.

"Genesis, nothing is going to happen to us.

I'm a lot stronger than you think. I can take care of myself. Would you rather me be in LA, worrying about you every second of the day."

"But you'll be safe in LA."

"How do you know that? If somebody is after you and they want to get to me, that can happen whether I'm in LA or in New York. At least if we're here you have a better chance of protecting us."

"I don't know, Skylar." Genesis got up from the bed and stood in front of the fireplace.

Skylar followed, standing behind him and placing her arms around his waist. She laid her head on his back as if she never wanted to let him go. "Please don't shut me out, Genesis. I want to be here with you."

"I know, but..."

"But nothing," Skylar interrupted. "As a precaution, we had already agreed that I would have my own place and not live with you. Nothing in your business has changed and neither should our decision. I'm very aware of the dangers that come with being in your life, but the risks are worth it to me. I love you and in my heart I know you will do everything to make sure me and my son are safe."

Genesis turned around and faced Skylar. He held her arms and stared deeply into her eyes. "Are you positive this is the life you want for you and your son?"

"If that life is with you then absolutely," Skylar said without hesitation.

"Then so be it."

"Thank you, baby. You'll see it will be the best decision you ever made." Skylar smiled before locking lips with Genesis for a long lingering kiss.

"Hi, Precious, it's me Amir. Did you make it back to New York yet?"

"Hey, Amir. No, I'm still in LA, but I'll be back tomorrow."

"I haven't heard from Aaliyah yet. What about you?"

"Yes, I did."

"You did?" Amir questioned sounding surprised.

"I apologize. I know how worried you've been. I should've let you know, but I thought Aaliyah would've called you too."

"Me too, but at least one of us heard from her. How did she sound?"

"She sounded pretty good. She's in Mexico."

"Mexico... why did she go to Mexico? Is she with Dale?"

"Not sure. She lost her cell phone. That's why she said she hadn't been in touch. The conversation was very brief, but she said she would call me again soon. She mentioned some people were waiting for her so that's why she couldn't talk long."

"Did Aaliyah at least say when she planned on coming back?"

"No, she said she wasn't sure. I'm waiting for her to call me back so I can get more answers. Honestly, I was so happy to hear her voice and know that she was okay that I didn't bombard her with a ton of questions."

"I understand. I'm glad she's okay too."

"Listen, I just got to Supreme's house. I came to see Xavier before I leave tomorrow. If Aaliyah calls, I'll make sure to tell her to call you."

"Thanks, Precious."

"No problem. I'll talk to you when I get back."

When Amir got off the phone with Precious he thought he would feel a sense of relief knowing that she had spoken to Aaliyah, but he didn't. "Aaliyah what is really going on with you?" he questioned out loud to himself. "You run off to Mexico in the midst of all this chaos. You did do that before, when you ran off to Miami," Amir reasoned. "But I thought you had grown past dumb shit like that. Or maybe I was wrong. Maybe you're the same self-absorbed Aaliyah you've always been." Amir punched his fist against the wall, frustrated that although they were no longer in a relationship, Aaliyah still had the capabilities to resonate so much anger in him.

Chapter Eight

Nothing But The Truth

"You're here early," Supreme said when he opened the door and saw a refreshingly stunning Precious standing there, in a blush pleated v-neck romper that had pintucked pleats encircling the waistline with nude colored sandals. One hand was placed in the two seam pockets as the other hand grasped her cream colored leather quilted Chanel clutch purse.

"I told you I wanted to spend the entire day

with our son before I headed back to New York tomorrow," Precious said walking in the foyer, knowing she looking like a glass of fine wine.

"I know. I just didn't expect for you to be here this early. We both know you're not a morning person."

"Oh, you remember that. Well, when it comes to Xavier, he's worth getting up for."

"He'll be happy you're here. He's looking forward to spending the day with you. So what do you have planned?"

"I thought I would let Xavier decide. I hope the first thing he wants to do is go have breakfast because I'm starving."

"Alan is finishing up cooking as we speak."

"Who is Alan?"

"The chef. I don't know why I thought you already knew that. But yeah, why don't you all eat here."

"I don't think Morgan would like that and to be real with you, I'm not interested in breaking bread with her either."

"I wouldn't expect anything less then for you to be honest about your feelings, Precious, but Morgan isn't here."

"Really, but doesn't she live here?"

"No. She stays here sometimes, but she has her own place."

"Oh, I guess she was marking her territory when she gave me the impression she lived here."

"Maybe," Supreme replied nonchalantly wanting to get off the Morgan subject. "So are you joining me for breakfast or not?"

"I would love to." Precious grinned.

"Wonderful. It's a beautiful morning, how about we eat outside by the pool," Supreme suggested.

"Sounds perfect, especially since this house has some of the best views in Beverly Hills."

"I'm sure you remember how to get to the back." Precious nodded her head yes. "Make yourself comfortable and I'll let Xavier know you're here."

Precious smiled to herself and for a brief moment it felt like old times again, when her and Supreme were so deeply in love. But she wouldn't let her mind go there because the last thing Precious wanted was a broken heart.

Dale was back in Miami, but his mind was stuck in New York. He couldn't get Aaliyah off his mind. The last time he saw her was at the restaurant when she rushed off to meet some realtor for her mom. It was a week later and was as if Aaliyah had vanished and Dale was about to lose his mind.

"Man, we're finally back in our city and you looking stressed. What's up wit' that," Emory commented putting down his car keys.

"I just need to get home."

"But we just got back from the airport. I thought you were going to hang out at my crib for a while."

"Not right now," Dale replied, clearly agitated.

"What's going on with you? You were quiet the entire flight. I thought you were tired because our flight was so early, but something is obviously wrong with you. What is it?"

"I don't wanna talk about it with you."

"What the fuck. Why would you say that to me? We brothers."

"Because I know how you feel about Aaliyah and I don't need that shit right now."

"I thought we were getting past that. Especially after I told her what I found out about that Arnez dude."

"Yeah, but that doesn't all of a sudden make you best friends."

"I understand that, Dale, but it does show that I'm trying. I know how you feel about Aaliyah and yeah I might not ever be best friends with her, but we are. You're not only my best friend, but more importantly my brother. So tell me what's going on with you?"

"I haven't heard or spoken to Aaliyah since she left the restaurant that day."

"Are you serious?"

"Very serious. I've been calling her nonstop. I went by her place and nothing. That's why I had us stay in New York for longer than we were supposed to. I was waiting to hear from Aaliyah." Dale sat down on the barstool as if defeated.

Emory studied Dale's face and it finally clicked that his brother wasn't frustrated because he couldn't get in touch with his girlfriend, he was scared. "Dale, you think some sort of foul play has happened to Aaliyah?"

"I don't want to, but why else would she just vanish without saying a word to me."

"Let's think about this for a minute. I mean, who would want to hurt Aaliyah?"

"You know her family is in the midst of a drug war and if your information accurate, Arnez Douglass is behind it. What if his next move was to take Aaliyah."

"No way. Trust me Dale, that ain't happening."

"How can you be sure? You know how cutthroat this game can be. No one is off limits when you go to war."

"True, but based on the moves he's been making, kidnapping hasn't been one of them. I think you're letting your fear get the best of you."

"Damn straight I am! I love that woman. If anything has happened to her, I will kill a motherfucker." Dale pounded down on the top of the bar. "I need to find her."

"You will and I'll help you. We're brothers... I got you. We'll find Aaliyah. I promise you," Emory said patting Dale's shoulder.

"Aaliyah, the more time I spend with you the more impressed I become," Arnez said taking a seat next to her.

"What is it, Arnez? I'm really not interested in having a conversation with you. I just want to watch television in peace. It's not like I have anything else to do."

"You can get back to your show after I'm done talking to you," Arnez said, picking up the remote and turning the television off.

"What the hell did you do that for! Gosh." Aaliyah rolled her eyes. "Say whatever you have to say so you can leave me alone."

"If you eased up you would realize that you

could learn a lot from me."

"Really? You think you can teach me more than my great father, Nico Carter, or my other father, the legendary Supreme. And let's not forget who I learned the most from, the baddest of them all, my mother, Precious Cummings. I'm sure you're very familiar with all three of those names. So if there is nothing else, you can go now."

"What I wouldn't give to break your neck."

"Then do it. Either kill me or leave me the fuck alone."

"I know after you got into Latreese's head, you're feeling overly confident in yourself, but you shouldn't."

"Got in Latreese's head?" Aaliyah frowned. "We can't stand each other. Remember you kept me tied up to make sure I didn't rip her face off."

"I do remember. That's why I was even more impressed that you were able to get a woman that hates your guts to open up and reveal all her dirtiest secrets. You played that very well."

"I don't know what you're talking about." Aaliyah shrugged.

"Yes, you do. I forgot to mention before I left, that this place is completely wired. I hear every sound, thought, and conversation," Arnez informed Aaliyah.

"So this place is bugged. Is that what you're saying?"

"That's exactly what I'm saying."

Aaliyah's face remained blank with no sign of emotion. She wasn't sure if Arnez was bluffing to get a reaction or if he was telling the truth.

"So you have nothing to say?" Arnez asked.

"Since you're able to hear everything then you should already know the answer to that."

"I've had a rough start today. I'm in no mood to play games so I'll get right to it. I know you convinced Latreese to spill it all to Amir. You're sitting there on that couch, thinking the entire crew will be coming to your rescue soon, but it ain't happening."

"Whatever you say," Aaliyah replied as if she didn't have a worry in the world.

"I can't figure out if you're really that arrogant, stupid, or just a bitch, but whatever it is, get comfortable because you will be staying for a lot longer."

Aaliyah watched with repulsion as Arnez got up and walked away. She wanted to snatch him up by his Polo V-neck and wrap it around his throat until he took his last breath. This wasn't the way shit was supposed to work out and now she needed another plan ASAP.

Fuck! This motherfucker would have this hole

in the wall wired. Leave it up to Arnez to want to be privy to every word spoken in this place. Before Latreese left I had gotten through to her and she had promised to tell Amir everything and tell him where I was being held captive. Now Arnez and Maya are going to do everything possible to stop her. Damn! Come on Latreese, don't give into them. Stand firm and come clean with Amir. You're the best chance I have of getting out of this dump and away from Arnez. Don't let me down, Latreese, I need you, Aaliyah thought to herself.

Latreese watched intently as Amir engaged in an intense conversation with someone on the other end of the phone. She welcomed the distraction as she built up her nerves to tell him everything she discussed with Aaliyah. Not only that, but that she also knew where Aaliyah was being held against her will. Latreese hadn't gotten any sleep and she knew it was time for her to take Aaliyah's advice and come clean. Her fear of losing Amir forever was what was holding her back, but the idea of Aaliyah ending up dead because she kept this information from Amir scared her even more.

Latreese never cared for Aaliyah, but it was mainly because she had everything that she always wanted... money, family, and Amir's love. It was more jealousy then dislike. But after Aaliyah listened and didn't judge her after she revealed her sordid past and questionable decisions, she developed a newfound respect for her nemesis. Latreese didn't want Aaliyah's blood on her hands and decided that doing the right thing was more important then enduring Maya's wrath or Amir cutting her out of his life for good.

"Babe, I need to talk to you about something," Latreese said when Amir got off the phone.

"Not right now, Latreese," Amir said abrasively as he started texting someone on his phone.

"But this is really important. It can't wait."

"Did you not hear what I said? I'm dealing with some heavy shit right now. Whatever you need to tell me can wait," he barked.

"This can't wait!" Latreese rushed towards Amir, adamant to get out what she needed to say, but he wasn't interested. Before she could utter another word, Amir received another call and he answered by the second ring.

"Why the fuck didn't you tell me that shipment didn't come in," Amir hollered over the phone. Latreese was mumbling in the background trying to get his attention, but he put his hand up dismissing her. He continued yelling at the person on the other end of the phone before walking out the room leaving Latreese alone.

While Latreese sat alone she began contemplating writing Amir a letter, confessing all her sins. She was beginning to feel desperate to expose her truth because if she didn't, her head would explode. As Latreese battled with herself, she noticed Maya was calling her phone. She ignored her call, but Maya became persistent.

"Stop calling! I'm not answering your call, Maya," Latreese sneered, slamming her phone down. Her anger was boiling over as Maya just kept calling her back to back. Right when she was tempted to answer the call and tell Maya to go to hell, she heard Amir's voice.

"I have to go."

"Amir, don't go. We really need to talk."

"I can't. I have to get to the warehouse before those dumbfucks make things worse. My father will kill me if I don't go make this shit right."

"Then let me come with you. We can talk during the ride," Latreese pleaded.

"Baby, I promise I won't be gone that long and we can talk about whatever you like then. But I have to go. And I'm sorry for yelling at you earlier. I have a lot of shit on my mind. I'll make it up to you when I get home. I promise," Amir said giving Latreese a kiss on the lips and walking out the door.

Latreese wanted to beg Amir to come back, but decided she would do as he asked and wait. To her relief she no longer feared telling him the truth instead she wanted him to know her story more than ever. Latreese poured herself a glass of wine and patiently waited for Amir's return.

Chapter Nine

Just Like Old Times

"Nico! It feels like I haven't seem you in years." Genesis gave Nico a man hug and patted him on the back a few time, happy to see his good friend and business partner. "Sit down. I hope you don't mind I already started eating. A brotha was starving." Genesis laughed. "Why don't you order something," he continued, sliding the menu over to Nico.

"I'm straight. I'm not hungry, but I will have a

drink." Nico waved over the waitress and ordered a Hennessey on the rocks.

"I might need me one of those, too," Genesis commented.

"Yeah, I should've ordered three. Between business and Precious, I think I grew a handful of gray hairs overnight."

"Man, I still can't believe Precious woke up on your honeymoon and got her memory back," Genesis shook his head before biting down on his steak.

"Who you telling. One minute she loves me, the next I'm like a stranger in her bed."

"Have you spoken to her since you've been back?"

"Not since I dropped her off at her place. I wanted to give her space. I'm sure she rushed off to see Supreme though."

"You think so?"

"Of course! That's who she woke up remembering to be the love of her life," Nico admitted angrily. "I can't wait for us to track down the people who ordered that hit at the warehouse. The person who got Precious shot is the one responsible for this madness. If she hadn't lost her memory, I would've never believed we had another chance at love. I mean I knew Precious would always hold a special place in my heart, but I had finally accepted that what we shared was over and moved on. I let myself fall in love with her all over again and now the joke's on me." Nico let out a heavy sigh.

"Man, you ain't neva nobody's joke. You're a good man and you'll find the right woman. Look at me. I've had so much bad luck with women, but without even meaning to I've met a woman that seems to fit me perfectly." Genesis smiled thinking about the last time he saw Skylar. She would be back for good in a couple days.

"I'm happy for you, Genesis. I'm glad Skylar makes you happy. If anybody deserves happiness, it's you. But I don't know if it's in the cards for me. First that Tori/Ashley situation and now Precious... I might need to be a bachelor for the rest of my life. No stress no headaches, 'cause I definitely don't need no more gray hairs." Nico chuckled. "But enough love talk. Let's get to what we're really here for... business or the lack there of. Any word on what's going on with that shipment?"

"Not yet. Amir is at the warehouse now checking on things. I'm hoping it's a simple misunderstanding, but...."

"But you think whoever is behind all the bullshit going on in our organization is responsible," Nico said finishing Genesis' sentence.

"Unfortunately yes. We definitely don't need this right now. Our money has already been funny these last few months with this drug war we have going on. If this continues we gon' be dried the fuck up."

"Maybe we need to head over to the warehouse. I mean you think Amir can handle things?"

"If not, he better learn quick. Hell, I'm ready to be like Quentin. Just sit back and collect money. You tryna keep the gray hairs from poppin' up, I'm tryna keep my hair free and clear of them, 'cause I ain't got one," Genesis jokingly bragged.

"Fuck you man!" Nico laughed.

"But seriously, I've been hustling in these streets, what feels like all my fuckin' life. Skylar is moving here with her son, who is very young. Of course, I want to step up and help her with him. She might even want us to have a child of our own. That means I'll have to slow shit down. Amir is a grown man now. He's intelligent, street savvy, knows the ins and outs of this business and more importantly, young enough to deal with all the headaches that come along with it."

"I feel you. I like Amir. I've been impressed with some of the business decisions he's made and how he conducts himself in doing so. But we both know how deadly this game is. One minute the world seems to be in the palm of your hand and the next, you don't know if you gon' live to see another day. You have to be built a certain way for this life. Do you think Amir is?" Nico questioned.

Genesis paused for a few seconds as if pondering Nico's question. "We will soon see now won't we," he said before finishing his dinner.

"Thank you for stopping by before going to the airport," Xavier said to Precious as she looked at him lovingly.

"You don't have to thank me. I'm your mother. Spending time with you is one of my greatest joys. I wish I could stay longer, but I was already supposed to leave three days ago and I need to get back to New York."

"I understand. I was glad you stayed the extra days. I felt like I finally had my mother back."

"I know it was hard on you, Xavier, when I lost my memory, but I never stopped loving you," Precious said holding her son closely. "You and your sister are the most important people in my life. I know things have been difficult for both of you, but I'm hoping this is a new beginning for all of us." Precious lifted his chin and smiled. "I still can't believe how tall you are and how handsome. You look exactly like your father." Precious' eyes began to tear up.

"Yep, with just enough of you in him, to make our son perfect," Supreme chimed in, catching both Precious and Xavier off guard.

"Dad, I thought you had left."

"I forgot something and had to come back. I'm glad I got to see you, Precious, before you went to the airport. Would you like for me to give you a ride?" Supreme offered.

"I have a driver waiting outside for me."

"Actually, I told him he could go ahead and leave."

"Then I guess I need that ride." Precious turned her attention back to her son. "Xavier, I hope you'll think about what I said."

"You mean coming to spend the summer with you in New York?"

"Yes."

"If it's okay with Dad, I would like that."

"Really!" Precious' face lit up.

"I think that's a great idea," Supreme agreed.

"Wow, I can't believe I'm going to have my handsome son with me for the entire summer. We're going to have so much fun. Aaliyah will be thrilled too. I can't wait to tell her. Now give your mom a hug before I go catch this flight." Precious held Xavier for a long embrace. "I love you, son," she whispered in his ear.

"I love you too, Mom."

Precious wiped the single tear falling from her eye and hurried off before she changed her mind about going back to New York again.

"I'll be back, son," Supreme said before following Precious to the car.

"It gets harder to say goodbye, doesn't it," Supreme stated once they both were in the car.

"Yes. It seems like yesterday I was carrying him on my hip and now he can carry me. Where does the time go?"

"I ask myself the same question. I look at him and can't believe he'll be eighteen soon. He'll be off to college, then one day he'll be married with children of his own."

"I'm looking forward to being a grandmother one day," Precious beamed.

"What! Not 'I'm-gonna-look-twenty-one-forever' Precious Cummings from Brooklyn," Supreme clowned.

"There are a lot of hot looking grandmothers out there. What you talkin' 'bout. I'll just be added to that list. People will be thinking my grandchild is actually my kid and I will gladly correct them," Precious teased.

"I'm sure. You might be looking forward to it, but I ain't ready for the grandfather title just yet. Hopefully Xavier and Aaliyah will wait a long time before they decide to have kids."

"I was a lot younger then Aaliyah when I had her. We were married and I just knew I was grown. You couldn't tell me a damn thing."

"Ain't nothing changed."

"Shut up!" She nudged Supreme with her elbow. "I think I've mellowed out nicely as I've gotten a few years on me."

"If you say so," Supreme countered, sounding unconvinced. "But I must agree with one thing," Xavier said.

"What's that?"

"It does feel like we have Precious back. It's been really nice having you here for the last few days. It seems like old times, when we never doubted how much we love each other."

"I know what you mean. That's why I was tearing up when I was saying goodbye to Xavier. It felt so right being there with the two of you, all we needed was Aaliyah. Speaking of Aaliyah, I haven't heard back from her."

"That's funny you say that because I called her and was going to leave a message, but her voicemail was full. I know you said she lost her phone, but I figured she would still be checking her messages."

"That's true. Let me call her phone now and see if her voicemail is still full." Precious put the call on speakerphone. After the greeting played the same message came through. "That's very strange. You would think she'd be checking her messages."

"And you haven't heard a word from Aaliyah since you spoke to her when we were in my office?"

"Nothing."

"That was almost a week ago. Something isn't right," Supreme said as he merged onto US-101 S. "I don't care if she's supposed to be in Mexico. Aaliyah may not call, but nothing keeps her from checking her voicemail, unless she can't."

"I agree. So what do you think we should do?"

"Tell me more about that Arnez situation. Is that a real verified threat or is it strictly speculation?" Supreme pried.

"Amir seemed pretty convinced it was real, but I don't think he has concrete proof."

"Then that's our next move. Finding out if Arnez is still alive."

"If Amir hasn't been able to find out what can we do?"

"My reach goes a lot further than Amir's. If

Arnez is truly alive then I will find him. That I can guarantee you." Supreme nodded as he changed gears in his silver Aston Martin DBS V8.

Chapter Ten

Your Time Is Up

When Amir arrived back at his place, all he wanted to do was take a hot shower, have a stiff drink, and lay back as Latreese gave him some magnificent head. His day was long and stressful as fuck. Nothing went right and everything that could go wrong did.

"Baby, I'm home. Sorry I'm getting back so late," Amir called out hoping that Latreese was still up waiting for him. He tossed his keys down on the kitchen counter and started unbuttoning his shirt before he even got halfway down the hallway. "Latreese, I know I said I would be home hours ago, but I promise to make it up to you," Amir said opening the bedroom door. *Damn, she probably in here knocked out,* Amir thought to himself; disappointed that if Latreese was sleep like he expected he wouldn't be getting any head before going to bed.

When Amir entered his bedroom there was loud music playing and it was pitch dark. He turned on the light switch and almost vomited when he saw Latreese's bloody body spread across his bed.

Amir ran over to Latreese and picked up the knife lying next to her body. Her body appeared to be motionless. "Latreese, you can't be dead! Who did this to you!" he mumbled, tossing down the knife and trying to lift her lifeless body.

Then he heard what were some inaudible words coming from Latreese. "I... I... I... have something to tell you," Latreese struggled to say.

"Shh," Amir whispered, gently placing his index finger over his finger. "Don't speak. You need to keep your strength. I'ma get you to the hospital," Amir said putting his arms around Latreese. Her blood had soaked through her once pastel purple dress and now drenched on Amir's shirt and pants.

"Wait," Latreese said so low that Amir could barely hear her. Her eyes kept shutting and then she would battle to slightly open them. "Aaliyah," she managed to get out.

Amir thought he heard Latreese wrong. "What did you say?"

"Aaliyah," she repeated.

"What about Aaliyah?" Amir was completely taken aback that out of all the people Latreese could mention as she barely clung to life, she would call out Aaliyah's name.

"Aaliyah..." Latreese uttered one last time before she died in Amir's arms.

"Latreese... Latreese... Latreese!" Amir howled over and over again. He began shaking her body, but Latreese was literally dead weight in his hands. He was transfixed in somehow miraculously bringing Latreese back to life that he ignored the knocking at the door.

The knocking got louder and louder until it became pounding. The relentless pounding still didn't get Amir's attention until he heard, "Police! Open the door! Open the door!"

Amir quickly scrutinized himself and he already knew what was about to happen next. As if predicting his future, he heard the front door being kicked open as the police rushed inside.

"Put your hands up! Put your hands up!" the officers shouted, pointing their weapons directly at Amir.

All Amir could do was shake his head. With ease he laid Latreese down and slowly put his hands up. He knew how bad it looked. He was caught holding his girlfriend's dead body, covered in her blood and had touched what he presumed was the murder weapon. In a blink of an eye, Amir's day had gone from bad to worse.

"I handled it," Maya boasted as she slid off from riding Arnez's dick.

"You damn sure did handle it like a champ." He smirked, smacking Maya's ass.

"I ain't talkin' 'bout yo' dick." Maya giggled. "I meant Latreese. She will no longer be a problem."

"I'm glad you got her under control. Next time I need her for babysitting duties tell her to make sure she keeps her mouth shut. Aaliyah is even smarter than I thought," Arnez said, lighting up a cigarette.

"Please... she ain't that smart. Besides we don't have to worry about Aaliyah influencing Latreese because she won't be doing any babysitting."

"Why not? I thought you got her in check," Arnez took another pull from the cigarette before passing it to Maya.

"Last I checked a dead person can't babysit," Maya responded before blowing o's with the smoke from the cigarette.

"What the fuck you mean dead?" Arnez rose up, leaning back on the headboard.

"I thought dead was a universal term."

"Are you stupid or something! Why the fuck would you kill that girl?" Arnez belted.

"Keep your voice down!" Maya growled. "That hoe was about to become a major problem so I eliminated her ass before it got to that point."

"We already in a fucked up situation 'cause we had to snatch up Aaliyah, now you out here committing an unnecessary murder."

"Unnecessary?! That silly broad was about to confess all to Amir. If I had let that bitch live one more minute she would've blown our cover."

"This shit is spinning outta control," Arnez huffed, reaching for another light. "Did you at least get rid of the body?"

"I did something even better."

"What?"

"I made sure to make it look like Amir killed Latreese. I waited and watched until I saw him arrive home. Then I placed an anonymous call letting the cops know I heard yelling and screaming coming from his apartment. I bet Amir is sitting in a holding cell as we speak begging his daddy to post his bail. Although I doubt they'll give him one." Maya laughed hysterically.

Arnez sat quietly, smoking his cigarette observing Maya. There was no doubt in his mind that she was quickly becoming a liability. He was beginning to regret that he didn't allow Aaliyah to put that bullet in the back of her head. Maya was impulsive and didn't think about the consequences of her actions. Arnez had meticulously planned out how he would execute every move against Genesis and his organization and things were moving along exactly as planned. In the beginning, Maya was a priceless asset. Her jealously and hatred for Precious made her a willing participant, but now she was taking shit way too far.

At that very instant, unbeknownst to Maya, Arnez decided her time was up and began plotting on how he would get rid of her once and for all.

Chapter Eleven

Guilt Trip

Aaliyah's days were becoming more and more repetitive. She spent the majority of her time plopped down on the same dusty couch watching the same shows over and over again. It had gotten to the point that the characters on Young And The Restless now seemed like personal friends. She began talking back to the television like they were having a meaningful in depth conversation.

"I don't know how much more of this I can

take. This place got me feeling dirty. I need a manicure and pedicure so fuckin' bad." She cringed, ogling her chipped polish. "If I don't get some sort of resolution soon to this madness, shit gon' get ugly," Aaliyah said out loud, but in a somewhat low voice. Now that she knew Arnez was listening to every word she said, she purposely kept the television turned up loud so he wasn't privy to her personal thoughts. Sometimes a girl wanted to vent to herself out loud without having to worry that someone was listening.

"Let me turn to Law & Order SVU and see what Detective Benson is up to," Aaliyah said, reaching for the remote to turn the channel from the news to the USA network. But before she got the opportunity she saw Amir's face plastered on the screen in a box shot and then actual footage of him being escorted out of this apartment in handcuffs by the NYPD.

"Amir Taylor is being charged with the brutal murder of Latreese Lawson," the anchorman reported.

"What the fuck! No! Could Latreese had come clean and Amir flipped out and killed her ass? Nah, that ain't Amir's style. That has Arnez's ass written all over it," Aaliyah seethed. As if right on cue, Arnez appeared from the back room, wearing some black sweats and a t-shirt, looking guilty as hell as far as Aaliyah was concerned.

"What you in here hollering about?" he questioned before catching the end of the report about Amir.

"You're responsible for that bullshit! You really are a piece of scum. Latreese didn't have to die and then to set Amir up to take the fall!" Arnez could practically see the steam coming from Aaliyah's head. "You fucked up with that move and I promise it's gon' bite you in yo' motherfuckin' ass," Aaliyah said with certainty.

"Watch yo' mouth lil' girl!"

"Fuck you old man!" Aaliyah spat, twisting her neck. "I ain't watching shit! At this point I'm 'bout ready for you to kill me, so I don't have to look at yo' ugly mug not a minute longer."

Arnez pierced his eyes deeply into Aaliyah to see if she was just having one of her daily tantrums or if there was some realness to her words. The light in her once sparkly, feisty eyes was starting to dim. The glow from her skin was now dull and her spirit was gloomy.

What the fuck did I expect? She's been in this dungeon for weeks now with no fresh air, no sunlight and it is taking a toll. This is not what I wanted. Damn Maya! Holding Aaliyah captive was not part of my plan. I can't even use her as a bargaining tool because it would expose me to danger, making me vulnerable to unwanted retribution. Now Latreese is dead and I have no idea how to clean shit up because I'm not ready to come out of hiding just yet, Arnez thought to himself.

"Listen, I had nothing to do with Latreese's murder or setting up Amir," Arnez said, trying to diffuse the bad blood as much as possible under the circumstances.

"You ain't gotta lie to me! Own up to yo' shit since you supposed to be such a big dog in the game."

"I don't have to lie to you and I'm not. Maya is the one that killed Latreese and made it appear that it was Amir."

"Wow! I believe you too. This does have Maya's ratchet ass written all over it. Both of ya going to hell," Aaliyah popped before turning off the television. She didn't want to hear anything else the news reporter had to say. Seeing Amir carried off in handcuffs triggered the horrific memories of one of the worst times in Aaliyah's life.

Aaliyah's wounds were still fresh from being locked up for the murder of Sway Stone and attempted murder of Justina. She was also set up, but the betrayal ran much deeper because Justina, a childhood friend, and her mother were the culprits. Now she had to watch Amir go through the exact same thing, but in some ways even worse. Aaliyah had no love for Sway Stone so although she knew she didn't kill him nor did she want him dead, she also wasn't tripping over his loss. Amir, on the other hand, did genuinely care for Latreese and might've even loved her.

"I know how close you are to Amir," Aaliyah heard Arnez say, snapping her out of her thoughts. "I also know you pretty much hate my guts. But for the record, I had absolutely nothing to do with Maya killing Latreese or placing the blame on Amir. If I had any inkling that she planned on making a stupid move like that, I would've put a stop to it."

"Again, I'm not surprised. I already called it. I told you Maya would be your downfall. Now you'll be able to witness firsthand just how destructive she can be."

"I know how to handle Maya."

"If you say so, but you sure don't seem confident to me. I wouldn't either though if my partner in crime was cuckoo for coco puffs Maya." Aaliyah shrugged.

"Like I said, Maya will be handled," Arnez snarled before storming off.

Aaliyah got a good laugh witnessing Arnez completely out of his element. She could tell he was used to being in control and people following his agenda. Aaliyah was damn near positive that Maya had been playing her role perfectly in the beginning. More than likely not only did she follow all of Arnez's rules, she did it with a smile on her face. Once Maya gained Arnez's trust and felt he needed her, she probably started showing her ass.

Yeah, Arnez, I bet you regretting your decision now. Maya is poison and anyone who aligns themselves with her will get infected, Aaliyah thought to herself as a devilish grin remained plastered across her face.

"Genesis, I just heard the news," Lorenzo said when Genesis answered the phone. "Man, I'm so sorry. How's Amir holding up?" Lorenzo inquired.

"Not sure, haven't been able to see him. The attorney I hired is at the police station now. My only concern at the moment is that they set bail so I can get him out. I don't want Amir to spend a day in jail, but that might be impossible," Genesis hated to admit.

"He's strong. Whatever happens, Amir can handle it. This is fucked up though. There's no way Amir would murder his girlfriend."

Genesis heard what Lorenzo was saying,

but he wasn't as sure. He knew what the wrong woman could drive a man to do. Latreese seemed like a nice girl, but from experience Genesis learned you could never be certain what was going on in two people's relationship. He didn't want to believe his son killed Latreese, but if he did, that wouldn't surprise him either. Regardless, Genesis would handle it and help Amir in any way possible. He was determined that no child of his would spend the rest of their life caged up behind bars, like an animal.

"I appreciate you saying that, Lorenzo."

"Of course. You've always had my back and I have nothing but love for Amir. You make sure you keep me posted on what's going on with him and if I can do anything to help."

"I will. Are you gonna still make the meeting this Friday?"

"Of course! I know how crazy business is right now. We have some serious executive decisions to make."

"Good. I know you've been going back and forth to LA to be with Dior so I wasn't sure if it was going to be a problem."

"Nah. Dior's straight. I'm not missing that meeting. I'll be there. But if you need to get in touch with me before Friday, I'ma phone call away. See you soon, man."

Not a second after Genesis got off the phone with Lorenzo someone was knocking on his door.

"Who could that be and why didn't the doorman call to let me know someone was on the way up?" Genesis questioned out loud as he walked to the door.

"Genesis, are you okay? How is Amir?" Precious questioned in a concerned and panicked voice. She brushed right past Genesis and came inside.

"I should've known it was you. Marco never calls when you stop by. He always just lets you up."

"Don't give him a hard time."

"He needs to get over that crush he has on you and do his damn job," Genesis said closing the door.

"Enough about Marco. What is going on with Amir? Do the police still have him?"

"Unfortunately, yes."

"Have you spoken to him to find out what happened? All I heard on the news was he was arrested for killing Latreese."

"I've only heard the same information as you. I'm waiting for his attorney to call me. He advised me to stay here and wait. He said it would be a media circus outside the police precinct and I didn't need to be caught up in that."

"I know it's difficult staying here when you want to be with Amir, but I agree with your attorney. He advised you right." Precious took a seat and placed her purse on the chair. "So what do you think happened? I know you've been speculating."

"I have, but honestly it doesn't make any sense. If they were having any problems in their relationship, Amir kept it from me. I saw him with Latreese the other day and everything seemed fine. I know he's been worried about Aaliyah, but..."

"You don't think Latreese's death has anything to do with Aaliyah's disappearance do you?" Precious jumped up and asked.

"Amir said you spoke to Aaliyah and she was in Mexico. He sounded like everything was fine. What's changed?"

"I did speak to her, but that was over a week ago and I haven't heard from her since. Not only that, her voicemail is full. That means she hasn't checked any of her messages. When I spoke to her she said she lost her phone, but that wouldn't stop her from being able to check her voicemail."

"So do you think something happened to her before or after you spoke to her?"

"Before I spoke to her. I think whoever has her made Aaliyah place the phone call to throw us off," Precious stated. After her conversation with Supreme on the way to the airport, Precious had spent the last couple days thinking of every scenario and that's the one that made the most sense to her.

"You might be on to something," Genesis said, leaning over the table, digesting everything Precious told him. "But if Aaliyah is still alive and they have her why hasn't the person made any demands? It's no secret that she comes from a very wealthy family."

"Maybe they don't want money," Precious reasoned.

"If not money then what? You think it's revenge?"

"I'm not sure. But for some reason I feel Latreese's death has something to do with it."

"What... why?" Genesis stared at Precious, puzzled.

"I don't know. But when I heard about what happened to Latreese on the news and when I got here and you mentioned Amir being worried about Aaliyah, I got this eerie vibe. I can't explain it. Maybe it's a mother's intuition. But..."

"Hold that thought," Genesis said, answering his phone. "Yes, send him up. Thanks. So you know, that was Marco letting me know Nico was on his way up," Genesis informed Precious.

"No problem, but I appreciate the heads up."

"Of course. I try to keep unnecessary drama to a minimum at all times."

"We all know you're the peacemaker, Genesis, and thank goodness. I can only imagine how crazy shit would be if we didn't have you to always wave the white flag."

"I guess you really do have your memory back." Genesis chuckled.

"Pretty much. There are some gaps and holes, but my doctor said that's to be expected. It will take some time before I remember everything, but bits and pieces are coming back."

"I'm happy for you. I know it must've... that must be Nico," Genesis said stopping mid-sentence to let Nico in. "Thanks for coming by," Genesis said letting him in.

"Of course. This is the type of situation that requires more than a phone call. I mean Amir locked..." Now it was Nico's turn to stop mid-sentence. His mouth dropped when he caught a glimpse of Precious. She was standing there in a simple white tank top, low cut denim jeans and a pop of color with a pair of Pierre Hardy four inch dark pink suede sandals with papaya trims and tasseled ankle ties. Her hair was in a high bun with a pink lippie that complimented her shoes. Part of Nico hated that he was still so drawn to her.

"Hello, Nico." Precious's tone was reserved and uninviting. "I'm glad you found the time to come see Genesis, but you couldn't respond to my text messages about our daughter."

"I was planning to text you back, but got sidetracked with some other things. I have spoken to Aaliyah and she said she was fine."

"You spoke to Aaliyah... when?" Precious perked up as optimism kicked in.

"Day before yesterday."

"What did she say?"

"That she was in Mexico. She had lost her phone, but wanted me to know she was fine and would call me again soon."

"Did she say when she was coming back home?"

"No and before we could really talk she said she had to go, but would call me later. I haven't heard back from her, but she's young and we all know that Aaliyah does have a tendency of taking off sometimes."

"Maybe," Precious huffed, "but something still doesn't feel right. You didn't pick up any vibes that something was off?"

"No. But honestly, Precious, I'm working through my own personal issues right now, so I probably wasn't as in tune with things as I might normally be. But I do believe our daughter is fine." Precious knew those personal issues Nico was speaking of had to do with her and she couldn't help but feel guilty.

"That's understandable," Precious said backing off her harsh tone.

"I think we should all be relieved that Nico heard from Aaliyah and it was recently. It sounds like it was a spare of the moment decision. Aaliyah decided she needed to get away and went to Mexico," Genesis stated, thinking that now they were all on one accord.

"You're probably right," Precious conceded. "When I spoke to her, Aaliyah did say that she knew I was on my honeymoon and she figured she would be back before us. We were supposed to be gone for almost two weeks. So that does make sense."

"No, it doesn't." Nico said, surprising both Genesis and Precious. They both stared at him with bewilderment.

"Nico, you just said that Aaliyah has a tendency of taking off which is true and that you believe she is fine. So why are you now saying what I said doesn't make sense?" Precious was curious to know.

"Because Aaliyah was aware that the honeymoon was over and we were on our way back to New York."

"Are you sure?" Precious' tone was now back in panic mode.

"Positive. I called her right before our plane

was taking off. She asked me what happened, but I told her I would talk to her about it when we got back. So I find it very odd that she told you she thought we were still on our honeymoon. Unless that was Aaliyah's way of discreetly dropping a hint that something isn't right," Nico rationalized.

"You might be on to something." Genesis nodded. "If someone does have Aaliyah, I'm sure when they had her make the phone call, they were listening so she could only say so much. Aaliyah knew that Nico was aware that he told her you all were on your way back."

"That's why Aaliyah made it a point of telling me otherwise because if I mentioned it to Nico, he would know something wasn't right," Precious said with that aha moment written on her face.

"Dammit!" Nico roared. Balling his fist as if it finally clicked Aaliyah had been taken. "Not this again. I can deal wit' a lot of bullshit, but Aaliyah missing isn't one of them," Nico said in an almost haunting voice.

Precious was much more composed in her reaction. No matter how much she tried to fight it and wanted to believe her free-spirited daughter had simply ran off to Mexico for a good time, something was indeed wrong. There was no denying it. Nico confirmed what Precious already knew deep down inside.

"If both of you can excuse me for a moment. This is Amir's attorney," Genesis let them know before disappearing into his office.

"What do we do?" Precious questioned as if Nico could miraculously resolve the problem with a simple answer.

"I don't know." The uncertainty in Nico's voice was troubling.

"That wasn't the response I was expecting."

"Precious, what do you want me to say? Don't worry, we'll find her... everything will be okay... I'll find a way to bring her home safely... No one will ever hurt our daughter, I'll make sure of that. Are those the things you expected me to say?" Nico stood with his hands in his pockets and waited for Precious to reply.

"You always have a plan or an idea of how to make everything right."

"No, you've proven to me that I don't have the power to make everything right."

"This isn't about us, Nico. Someone has taken our daughter. What are we going to do to get her back?"

Before Nico could answer, Genesis came back into the room. "The good news is the attorney was able to get bail, but Amir has to stay in jail until tomorrow. But he'll be in a holding cell," Genesis said, sounding somewhat relieved.

"That's a start," Nico said patting Genesis on his back.

"Was the attorney able to give you any more information surrounding Latreese's death?" Precious inquired.

"No, he kept the conversation strictly about bail. I'll have to wait until I speak to Amir tomorrow to find out what happened."

"And if Latreese's death has anything to do with Aaliyah's disappearance," Precious added. She prayed they would finally get some answers soon because Precious' gut told her that time would be the deciding factor whether they would find Aaliyah dead or alive.

Chapter Twelve

The Set Up

Maya entered the upscale restaurant on Madison Avenue wearing a Givenchy white necktie blouse, contrasting panel trousers and some ankle cuff sandals with gold hardware. Her freshly trimmed, chin-length jet black bob accentuated her oval face perfectly. You would never know that the meticulously groomed woman was a charismatic psychopath.

What exactly defined a charismatic psychopath? In one word: a liar. They could be irresist-ible, charming, believed their own lies, extremely persuasive, and also have the ability to manipu-late well. So when Maya sat down to have lunch with her father, Quentin, she was in full charis-matic psychopath mode.

"Daddy, I'm so happy to see you. I missed our weekly lunches." Maya smiled lovingly.

"I have, too. I wasn't expecting to need to deal with some business that would keep me away for a couple weeks."

"I hope you were able to take care of every-thing," Maya said in her most concerned voice.

"I was." Quentin nodded.

"Good. You know I worry about you, Daddy. I almost lost you one time. I don't think I could handle almost losing you again."

"You don't have to worry about that," Quen-tin reassured Maya, putting his hand over hers. "I'm taking very good care of myself. I want to do everything necessary to be here for my kids and grandkids."

"Speaking of your kids, have you spoken to Precious?"

"No. I didn't want to disturb her while she was on her honeymoon. I'm sure her and Nico are back now, but I wanted to give the newlyweds some time to get settled into the married life.

Have you spoken to your sister?"

"Yes, I have. She cut her honeymoon short. Precious is also back to not claiming me or better yet, hating me."

"What?" Quentin tossed his napkin down totally caught off guard by what Maya said. "The two of you were on good terms when she left for her honeymoon."

"That was before she got her memory back."

"Precious got her memory back?"

"Sure did."

"I'll be damned! Maybe that's the reason Precious came back early from her honeymoon. I go away for a couple weeks and come back to all these changes," Quentin said shaking his head. "So now your sister wants nothing to do with you." He frowned.

"Worse then that, she accused me of harming my niece. As if I would ever do anything to hurt Aaliyah." Maya gave a convincing dejected stare that made Quentin sympathize with his youngest daughter.

"Has something happened to Aaliyah?" Quentin's eyes widened.

"Not that I know of. I mean, Precious and Amir showed up at my apartment. Let themselves in with the key you gave her. I had just gotten out of the shower so I was standing in my towel while they interrogated me. I told Precious I hadn't seen or spoken to my niece. They searched every inch of my apartment and found nothing, but that wasn't good enough for my sister." Maya sighed. "She threatened to kill me, but not before shoving my head against the wall and choking me."

"What... are you serious?"

"Yes. I thought we made so much progress, but with her memory back it's all gone out the window."

"I'm so sorry you had to go through that, Maya. I'm going to talk to Precious. I also want to find out what is going on with Aaliyah. But if something had happened to my granddaughter I would think Precious would've called me. After I leave here, I'll be going to have a conversation with Precious to find out what the hell is going on."

"Daddy, you need to calm down. It wasn't my intention to upset you. I thought you should know what has been going on since you've been gone. I also hoped that you could help mend my relationship with Precious. I love her so much and I would hate not being in my sister's life."

"Don't you worry, Maya. We both know how stubborn Precious can be, but I will do everything in my power to make things right between the two of you."

"Thank you, Daddy." Maya got up from her chair and embraced her father. He welcomed his daughter's warm hug as Maya smiled behind his back plotting her next move.

"Amir, I need for you to tell me the truth. If you lie to me, I can't help you. For whatever reason, if you killed Latreese it's essential you tell me exactly what happened. Don't put us through a long futile trial if you know the prosecutor will have evidence to put you away for the rest of your life. If we act now, I'm still in a position where I might be able to make this go away, but I have to know what I'm up against," Genesis explained to his son.

Amir stood on the private terrace of his father's penthouse, looking over the stone banister, watching the sun pass through the sky as the morning breeze hit his face. For a brief moment, he was able to find peace in what had turned into the most chaotic time of his life. Amir was being charged with murdering his girlfriend and now his father was asking him did he do it.

"Dad, out of everybody I was hoping you would be the one person who wouldn't ask me that question."

"Son, I know from personal experience what the wrong woman is capable of making a man do. I'm not here to judge you, I'm here to save your life."

"I know, but I didn't kill Latreese. I swear on everything I love which includes the mother I never knew."

"I believe you," Genesis said hugging his son. "So tell me what happened."

"I came home. It was late because I had been at the warehouse all night trying to sort out that mess with our shipment. When I came home the music was on in the bedroom and I found Latreese barely alive in a pool of blood in the bed."

Genesis could see the color drain from Amir's face as he remembered what he witnessed that night. "I understand how painful this has to be for you."

"Dad, Latreese died in my arms. I held her as she took her last breath. I don't understand how anyone could do that to her."

"You said she was barely alive when you found her. Did she have a chance to say anything to you before she died?" Genesis questioned.

Amir hesitated, turning to stare over the banister again.

"What is it, Amir? Did Latreese tell you

something?"

Amir let out a deep sigh. "I haven't told anyone this, but she said Aaliyah's name."

"Aaliyah?"

"Yes. First she mumbled that she had something to tell me. Then she said Aaliyah's name. Dad you don't think she had anything to do with Latreese's murder do you?" Before Genesis could answer, Amir kept talking. "I mean, I could never imagine Aaliyah doing something like that and I feel guilty for even thinking it. But I haven't spoken to her in weeks and then she supposedly ran off to Mexico." Amir couldn't contain the confusion, frustration, and anger in his voice. "None of it makes any sense."

"Aaliyah didn't kill Latreese," Genesis stated.

"I want to believe that, but how can we be sure?"

"Because Aaliyah didn't run off to Mexico, she's been kidnapped."

"No! This is turning into a never-ending nightmare. Do you have any idea who has her?"

"We're not sure."

"What if that is what Latreese was trying to tell me?"

"But how would Latreese know who took Aaliyah? They're not even friends."

"I don't know, but..." Amir went silent as the

wheels began turning in his head. He replayed those final words a dying Latreese spoke to him. Then he decided to rewind even more and recalled the last conversation they had before he left to go to the warehouse.

"But what... do you remember something?"

"Latreese said there was something really important she wanted to talk to me about. She was being so persistent, but I brushed her off because I was on the phone arguing with one of our workers. When I told her I had to leave she even asked if she could ride with me so we could talk. Damn! If only I had listened or let her come with me," Amir choked up. "Fuck! Latreese would still be alive."

"You don't know that. Please don't blame yourself. All you're doing right now is speculating."

"No, it makes sense," Amir said clapping his hands together. "I bet you whatever Latreese was trying to tell me before I left had something to do with why she was killed. And Dad, my attorney said that one of the detectives told him they received an anonymous call from a neighbor saying they heard a woman scream and loud arguing coming from my apartment. But that was a lie because when I got home Latreese was basically already dead. The music was turned on and within minutes of me being home, the police were kicking down my front door."

"Like you had been set up," Genesis said.

"Exactly. Whoever killed Latreese set me up to take the fall. I bet if we find Latreese's killer, we'll find the person responsible for kidnapping Aaliyah too."

Chapter Thirteen

She's The Devil

"Hello, Quentin," Precious said letting her father inside her condo. "This visit is very unexpected."

"I don't know why. I've been trying to get in touch with you for days now, but you haven't returned my calls. You left me no choice but to pop up. Mind you, this is my third time doing so. The other two times you weren't home."

"I have a lot going on. I'm trying to get Xavier's room prepared because he's spending the summer with me."

"That's wonderful, Precious. I can't wait to spend some quality time with my grandson." Quentin smiled.

"I'm sure Xavier will enjoy that, too."

"Yes, indeed. This will be a great summer. I'll be able to spend time with Xavier and Aaliyah."

Precious seemed to ignore Quentin's comment and began going through some mail on the kitchen counter. "Can I get you anything to drink," Precious offered, not taking her eyes off the mail she was holding.

"No, I'm good. So how is my granddaughter? I've been trying to get in touch with her too, but I guess Aaliyah really does take after her mother because she isn't returning my calls either."

"You sure I can't get you anything, Quentin?"

"Positive. But what you can do is tell me where my granddaughter is."

Precious finally took her eyes off the mail and made contact with her father. Like a true gangster, he was clean, wearing an expensive suit and tie as if he was just leaving the office of his Fortune 500 CEO executive position. At first glance, many would think Quentin's eyes were made of stone. But upon further reflection, you could see he had a heart of gold and deep down, Precious knew that too.

"Aaliyah has been kidnapped," Precious divulged. She wasn't in the mood to talk in circles with her father. She figured it was best to get it out in the open.

"How long ago did this happen?"

"A few weeks, but it's only been about a week since we pretty much confirmed it."

"You know how close I am to Aaliyah. Don't you think you should've told me?"

Precious could hear the anger in her father's voice and she did sympathize with him, but unfortunately, he played for the wrong team.

"I get that you're upset, but I didn't want you running back telling Maya anything we discussed about Aaliyah."

"You can't possibly think your sister has anything to do with Aaliyah's disappearance."

"I don't know what to think. We have no idea who has Aaliyah. But I don't trust Maya, so regrettably, I can't trust you."

"Are you serious?"

"Very! Maya is the enemy. I've given her chance after chance and the only reason why is because of you. If you weren't her guardian angel, Maya would be dead by now. But I can promise you this. If I find out Maya had anything to do with my daughter's disappearance, you won't be able to save her, Quentin. Sister or no sister, I will personally kill Maya myself."

"Stop this foolishness right now! Nobody is killing anybody!" Quentin declared. "Maya had nothing to do with what happened to Aaliyah. She loves her niece just like she loves you. I guess now that you've gotten your memory back you've forgotten all the progress we've made as a family."

"Let me guess, Maya told you I got my memory back because I damn sure haven't had the opportunity to. And while Maya was spilling that info to you, I'm sure she had those big crocodile tears in her eyes, begging you to plead her innocence to anyone that would listen."

"Maya didn't have to beg for anything because I know my daughter is innocent, it's sad that you don't."

"I'll tell you what's sad. Maya has you so completely hypnotized that you can't even recognize when the devil is standing right in front of your face. But that will be your downfall, not mine."

"I truly believed we were past all of this. In a way, I thought when you lost your memory it was somewhat of a blessing in disguise. It gave us all an opportunity to start over with a clean slate. For those few months, it was the closest I ever felt to you. You had finally let down that guard that no matter how hard I tried, you kept up. You even called me Dad. I finally believed that you loved and accepted me as your father. Now, I'm just back to being Quentin. A man that you treat like a stranger."

"I do love you, Quentin, but you refuse to see Maya for the dangerous, conniving psycho that she is. I have to protect my family and myself. If Maya is my family's enemy, then anybody that affiliates with her is my enemy, too."

"I understand the importance of family so I get where you're coming from. As your father, can you do this one thing for me?"

"What is it?"

"When you find out that Maya had absolutely nothing to do with Aaliyah's disappearance, will you make a sincere effort to build a relationship with her as your sister.

"Quentin I... I..." Precious mumbled, unwilling to agree to her father's request.

"It's the least you can do for me. When you see that I'm right about Maya, that can be your way of apologizing for being wrong without actually having to say I'm sorry to an old man." Quentin gave Precious an endearing smile.

"For the record, even if Maya has absolutely nothing to do with Aaliyah's disappearance, it doesn't change my feelings towards her. But if I'm wrong, I will make an effort, but only because

I do love you."

"Thank you." Quentin walked over to Precious and kissed her on the forehead. "And don't you worry, Precious, we will find Aaliyah alive."

"I needed to hear you say that." Precious got teary-eyed for the first time since finding out Aaliyah was missing. She wanted to remain strong, but the fear had been building up and she was slowly releasing it. Quentin held his daughter tightly wanting Precious to feel secure. "I wanted to hear those words from Nico, but he couldn't say them. That scared me more than anything because Nico always had this way of making me believe that when he put his mind to it, he could make everything right."

"Don't be so hard on Nico. He's scared too and that's not easy for a man like him to admit. Aaliyah is his only child. The very idea of losing her is probably more agonizing than anything he's ever experienced in his life."

"I'm sure you're right."

"When tragedy strikes, that is the time when being united not only as parents, but husband and wife is the most crucial."

"Nico and I aren't in a good place right now," Precious admitted, releasing herself from Quentin's arms.

"Aaliyah's disappearance has ripped the two

of you apart already?"

"No, it has nothing to do with that."

"Then what?" Quentin was quickly able to decipher what happened, as the answer hit him right after he asked the question. "When you got your memory back, you no longer wanted to be married to Nico," he said.

"How crazy is that. Nico is the last person I wanted to hurt. When I woke up on that beautiful island, the only man I expected to see in the bed next to me was Supreme."

"The heart wants what the heart wants," Quentin said as if reflecting on his own life.

"The even crazier part is that my heart wants Supreme, but his heart doesn't want me."

"I wouldn't be so sure about that. You and Supreme share a long, complicated history. That sort of love is always one second away from being reignited. But then I can easily say the same thing about you and Nico."

"True, but my love life has to be put on the backburner for now. All my time and energy has to go into finding Aaliyah. I was even considering not letting Xavier come so I could focus on that, but I decided having my son here would be good for both of us."

"I agree. Xavier needs his mom and you need him too. You'll be amazed how having him here will give you all the strength you need to bring Aaliyah home."

"Aaliyah has to come home because if she doesn't, none of our lives will ever be the same."

"Is this really necessary!" Aaliyah snapped as Arnez tied her up. "Where the hell am I going to go?"

"I'm so close for my well-executed plan to come full circle that I can't take any chances of you fucking it up."

"I'm not the one you need to worry about fucking it up. It's Maya you better be keeping in your back pocket."

"Maya is being dealt with."

"If you say so. But umm, can you at least leave the television on while you're gone?"

"Sure," Arnez said, turning the television to the ID Channel since he knew Aaliyah enjoyed watching their shows. "I won't be gone that long and if you behave yourself, I'll even bring you back some of that pizza you like."

It hadn't gone unnoticed by Aaliyah that recently Arnez had been somewhat amiable towards her. Although he tried to be subtle, it struck Aaliyah as odd that her captor was trying to make her stay a tad bit more comfortable. It started with Arnez asking and then buying some of her favorite foods to eat. Then he provided her with more girl-friendly hair and hygiene products. When he gave her a DVD player with a handful of movies she wanted, Aaliyah was convinced Arnez was up to something. She wasn't sure if he was planning to kill her soon and wanted to make her last days as comfortable as possible or if there was another reason that triggered his sudden need to accommodate his prisoner.

Aaliyah was baffled with Arnez's sudden change in behavior. The uncertainty of his next move had her on edge. She was beginning to think the time had come where it was either kill or be killed. So Aaliyah began planning her own escape and if Arnez had to die in the process then so be it.

Chapter Fourteen

Look Me In The Eyes

Gomez Vargas was sitting at the bar in his after hours lounge reading the New York Post. It was a daily ritual he had, when he stopped by during the afternoon hours to make sure his staff was properly preparing for opening later that night. As he leaned back, flipping through the pages in the paper, he instantly stopped when he recognized the face of one of his most prized former workers.

"Kendra is dead," he said out loud, studying the black and white photo they had of Latreese in the top left corner of the page.

Gomez read the article carefully and two things stood out to him. Kendra's name was listed as Latreese Lawson and her boyfriend Amir Taylor had been charged with her murder.

"Amir Taylor... why does that name sound so familiar to me?" Gomez questioned, continuing to talk to himself out loud. The bartender who was doing a liquor count wasn't paying her boss any attention as this behavior was normal for him until the picture in the newspaper article he was reading caught her eye.

"Is that Kendra?" she questioned getting a closer look at the picture.

"Sure is. She was murdered."

"That's a damn shame. She was a sweet girl," the bartender remarked then went back to doing her work.

Gomez continued reading the article over and over again. He hadn't seen or heard from Kendra since the day he sold her to Maya over two years ago. Gomez never forgot the woman he always referred to as his favorite girl. He often thought about the day he stole her virginity at the tender age of fifteen. Now the woman he still thought of as his personal property was dead and Gomez wanted to know more about the man accused of killing her.

Dale and Emory arrived in New York with two different agendas. Emory wanted to close a deal with a new connect and meet with his silent partner Arnez. Dale, on the other hand, came to get answers about Aaliyah whom he hadn't seen or heard from in nearly two months.

"Where do you want our driver to take you first?" Emory asked as they made their way through JFK Airport towards baggage claim.

"You go ahead; I'm getting a rental car," Dale informed his brother.

"Why? We can ride together."

"Because I won't be handling any business with you today. I wanna try to make contact with Aaliyah's family. I haven't been able to get in touch with anyone and I need answers. I have to find out what happened to my girlfriend."

"I'll come with you. I wanna help, Dale."

"I appreciate that, but I have to do this on my own. I don't need any distractions."

"I feel you. Will you be able to make our meeting tomorrow night? I think it's important you be there to close the deal with this new connect."

"I'll be there."

"Are you sure?" Emory pushed, not convinced his brother would show up.

"I said I'd be there!" Dale barked. Business was the furthest thing on his mind and hearing his brother talk about it was pushing Dale's buttons.

"Calm down. I'm not tryna upset you. I know how hard Aaliyah's disappearing act has been on you."

"What the fuck you mean her disappearing act?" Dale's face frowned up, mean mugging his brother. "You sayin' you think Aaliyah decided out the blue to just say fuck Dale I ain't dealing wit' him no more. Is that how you think shit went down... huh? Speak up motherfucker!" Dale was up so close on Emory that they were basically sharing the same space. People passing by were beginning to stare at the brothers and Emory was not feeling the unwanted attention.

"Yo, Dale, calm the fuck down," Emory said, easing back trying to put some space between them. "I apologize. I used a poor choice of words. Never did I mean to insinuate that Aaliyah had said fuck you."

Even after trying to explain himself, Emory wasn't able to diffuse the situation. Dale was on ten and he had to calm his brother down before they both ended up getting arrested on some dumb shit.

"Look, this ain't the time or place for this, Dale," Emory spit, putting on his own mean mug. I apologized, let's leave at that."

"I'll see you tomorrow," Dale snarled and headed in the opposite direction.

"Yeah hello," Emory grumbled, answering his phone as he watched Dale storm off.

"You a'right?" Arnez questioned, hearing the tension when Emory answered.

"I'm straight... what's up."

"I was checking to make sure you arrived in New York and we're still on for today."

"Yep, I'm at the airport now. I'ma check into my hotel and then I'll meet you at our spot."

"Cool, I'll see you then."

Emory was glad Arnez kept their conversation short because his mind was on his brother. The situation with Aaliyah had his head fucked up and Emory was afraid that if Dale didn't find her soon, their business would begin to suffer.

"Damn, Aaliyah, where the fuck are you," Emory mumbled walking towards his awaiting car.

"Daddy, what a pleasant surprise," Maya beamed, giving her father a hug. "Come on in. What brings you by, although you don't need a reason to visit me."

"That's good to know. It's nice to know my presence is welcomed," Quentin said.

"Always! Sit down, I was just eating some popcorn about to watch a movie, but I much rather talk to you."

Maya was stretched across the couch with her legs folded. She had on some pink and black Victoria's Secret boy shorts and a matching tank top. Her fresh face and bright smile made her appear to be any father's ideal daughter.

"I'm glad you're in a talkative mood because there are some things I wanted to discuss with you."

"Sounds serious," Maya said, putting her popcorn down on the table.

"It's about your sister. I spoke to her recently about you."

"I'm sure that didn't go well."

"We made some progress."

"Oh really? That's surprising."

"Precious does have some reservations

especially when it comes to Aaliyah."

"What about Aaliyah?"

"My granddaughter is missing."

"What! Somebody took Aaliyah... who and why?" Maya asked in her most convincing shocked and alarmed voice.

"Nobody has the answers to those questions yet, but if I have anything to do with it, we will very soon."

"If anybody can get to the bottom of it, it's you. For Aaliyah's sake, I hope you get those answers soon."

"Do you mean that, Maya?"

"Of course, how can you even ask me that?"

"Precious is convinced that you have something to do with Aaliyah's disappearance... do you?"

"I can't believe this. Precious has finally turned you against me too," Maya sniveled as her eyes filled with fake tears.

"I haven't turned against you, Maya. All I want to do is get to the truth. You're my daughter and no matter what, I'll always love you, but wrong is wrong and right is right. If Precious is correct, I need you to make this right and tell me where my granddaughter is."

"Daddy, are you asking me or have you already decided I'm guilty?"

"Are you guilty?"

"Daddy, I want you to look me in the eyes and listen very carefully." Maya was now down on her knees looking up at her father as if she was an innocent child being wrongly accused.

"I have absolutely nothing to do with Aaliyah's disappearance. I would never hurt her. I made a lot of mistakes in the past because I listened to my brother and did whatever he told me to do. I was young and stupid then, but I'm not that person anymore. You coming into my life changed all that. I know that you love Precious. I only hope that you won't let your desire to be close to her stop you from loving me because I'm your daughter too."

"Of course not," Quentin reassured her. He wrapped his strong arms around Maya, feeling that he needed to protect her. "I defended you with all my might to Precious, but I had to be sure I was standing up for the right person. Thank you for letting me know that I am," he said squeezing her tightly.

"I hope so. I've done everything to prove I've turned my life around, but I'm constantly being judged for my past. Everybody else gets a second chance, at what point do I get one too."

"Now it's my turn to have you look me in the eyes," Quentin said holding Maya's face up with his hands. "I've seen you turn your life around and I'm so proud of you. Sometimes it takes other people a little longer to see the change, like your sister. But Precious made me a promise, that when I prove to her you had nothing to do with what happened to Aaliyah, she will make a sincere effort to have a meaningful relationship with you."

"Precious really said that?"

"Yes, she did. When we find Aaliyah and bring her home, Precious will realize that she was wrong about you. Then the two of you can finally work on having a loving relationship as sisters. That's what I want more than anything."

"I want that too, Daddy."

I do believe Precious and I can finally have a meaningful sisterly relationship, but unfortunately for you, Daddy, that means your beloved Aaliyah has to stay gone. There's no way I can let you find your granddaughter alive because then you'll discover all my lies and realize Precious isn't wrong about me. I can't let that happen, but I promise to hold your hand and console you at Aaliyah's funeral, Maya thought to herself while her father continued holding her.

Chapter Fifteen

The Great Escape

Aaliyah watched carefully as Arnez prepared to leave. She studied his every move, specifically where he retrieved his keys, something she had been focusing on a lot lately. Aaliyah noticed that before Arnez would leave and every time he returned, he would place the keys in the same spot. Those keys represented her freedom and Aaliyah wanted to make sure she knew exactly where they were located when it was time to make her escape.

"I see you're going out again. I guess that means it's time for me to get tied up," Aaliyah said extending her arms.

"You can put your arms down. I won't be tying you up today."

"Did I hear you right... no cuffs?"

"No cuffs. I've triple checked this place and there's no way to get out without these," Arnez said, dangling his keys. "And since they'll be with me, you're stuck. But don't do nothing stupid or this will be the last time you'll enjoy being able to walk around freely while I'm gone."

"Don't worry you can trust me. I'll just be here watching a movie and staying out of trouble."

"I'll try not to be gone too long," Arnez said, holding on tightly to his keys and leaving out.

Arnez laughed while walking to his car thinking about Aaliyah because the more time he spent around her the funnier she was to him. He knew the moment he walked out the door she was scheming on what she could get into. The reason Arnez could laugh about it was because he had taken every precaution to make sure there wasn't shit for her to find. But leaving her handcuff free was also Arnez's way of testing her. He couldn't wait to get back to see if Aaliyah would pass or fail.

As Arnez made his way to Staten Island

to meet with Emory he noticed that Maya was calling him. He had been ignoring her a lot lately as he was trying to distance himself. But Arnez hadn't decided exactly how he planned on ridding himself of Maya so he didn't want to raise her suspicions until he did.

"What up, Maya," Arnez answered, trying to make it seem that everything was cool between them.

"You tell me what's up. I've been trying to get in touch with you for the last few days and you've been ignoring me. Why is that, Arnez?"

"Shit been crazy. You know I'm working diligently to bring this plan together."

"I thought we were working together. When did this become a solo project?"

"Maya, why you trippin'. You know what I meant. Of course we partners in this."

"Just making sure. So where are you now?"

"On my way to handle some business for us." Arnez stressed the word us for Maya's benefit.

"What about Aaliyah, you left her alone?"

"Yeah, but she's straight. I got everything extra secure over there. She ain't gettin' out."

"Cool. Well, I'm not going to hold you up, but we need to get together later on this week. We have some business to discuss."

"Then later this week it is. Let me know what

day is good for you."

"I will. Talk to you later, Arnez."

Arnez hung up with Maya and immediately wished he could get rid of her ass today. But he had to remain patient because the time wasn't right. Arnez remembered when he first made contact with Maya. He had remained underground allowing everyone to believe he was dead except for a couple of trusted and loyal workers. Arnez sent them to retrieve some money he had hidden. It wasn't the sort of money Arnez was used to, but it was enough for him to maintain and get his foot back in the drug game. To remain in the shadows, Arnez had his workers become the face of his operation, but there was no doubt who was in charge behind the scenes.

It took time and persistence, but eventually Arnez built up a solid operation that was becoming lucrative. But Arnez had bigger goals than simply stackin' paper, he wanted revenge on the one person he felt responsible for everything that had went wrong in his life... Genesis Taylor. He continued to be the motivation for every move Arnez made. He was determined to destroy Genesis, but he knew he couldn't do it alone. Arnez needed help and it couldn't just be anybody. It had to be someone with access to Genesis' inner circle and that's when Arnez set his sights on Maya.

Maya didn't have a direct link to Genesis, but she was within touching distance of people that did, mainly her father, Quentin. When Arnez presented Maya with the opportunity to make money, gain power, and cause havoc she couldn't resist. But what started off as a mutually beneficial partnership had turned into a power struggle and Arnez had no intentions of letting Maya win.

Nico, Genesis, Quentin, Amir, Lorenzo, and Precious sat around the boardroom conference table going through all the paperwork given to them from the three different private investigators they had hired. Most of it was vague and gave them no deeper insight into who was responsible for the nonstop mayhem that continued to plague their organization.

"Whoever is running the show has done an excellent job of covering their tracks," Lorenzo was the first person to look up and state.

"I've read over these papers multiple times and this shit still ain't making no sense to me," Quentin threw up his hands and said.

"Yeah, nothing is adding up. I thought the

investigator had some concrete proof that Arnez was the person behind this," Amir added.

"Not only Arnez, but also that Maya had been helping him," Precious said. "All of this is hearsay from some third person who isn't even using their real name."

"This is a real letdown," Nico said pushing the papers to the side. "It's like we have to go through ten different people and then five more, but even after that we still don't see who the main guy is. What type of ghost are we fighting?"

"That ghost is Arnez," Genesis stated as if there wasn't a doubt in his mind.

"How can you be sure? I know this bullshit we just got done reading couldn't have convinced you of that," Lorenzo huffed. "How much did we pay these fuckin' investigators anyway for this garbage."

"It has nothing to do with what's in these reports, it's what's not in them. If you supposed to be dead of course you gon' have other motherfuckers making moves for you. What better way to attack then in silence? Arnez has turned himself into an untouchable ghost," Genesis said in frustration.

"For argument's sake let's all agree that Arnez is the one behind the scenes calling out the shots. Let's even take it a step further and agree that he is the one who has Aaliyah. The question remains, how do we find him?" Lorenzo wanted to know.

"I would say we start with one of the low level workers who gave these investigators some of this hearsay information," Nico suggested.

"That might work," Amir agreed. "I mean like they say where there's smoke there's fire. These people may not have seen Arnez personally, but they might be able to give us the name of the person who has."

"Check this out," Nico said flipping one of the papers over. "Two different workers, somebody named Bobbie and the other Daryl mentioned the same man... Gomez Vargas."

"Yeah, but they never say this Gomez character knows Arnez," Quentin points out.

"True, but both of them said they first heard the name Arnez mentioned from this Gomez guy. That can't be a coincidence. Maybe he doesn't know Arnez, but what if he has an association with someone that does," Nico implied.

"You might be on to something with that, Nico," Precious spoke up and said. "I think we need to find out who this Gomez Vargas is and why he would be mentioning a man that's supposed to be dead."

"I agree," Genesis chimed in.

"Me too." Lorenzo nodded his head along

with Amir and Quentin.

"Glad we're all in agreement. We'll do a thorough background check on Mr. Vargas and see where it leads us. I think we've covered everything, unless anyone else has something to add." Genesis made eye contact with each person around the table.

"I think we're good," Lorenzo said when Genesis got to him.

"Then I'll see each of you here next week at the same time, unless something comes up and we need to call an emergency meeting," Genesis said standing up.

"How are you holding up?" Nico came around the table and asked Precious as everyone began to make their exit.

"Taking it one day at a time. Xavier will be here tomorrow so I think that will be good for me."

"For sure. I have to go to Miami for a few days, but if you need anything, you can always call me."

"I know we aren't on the best of terms right now, so it means a lot to hear you say that. Thank you, Nico."

"We're parents first and our mutual love for Aaliyah will always supersede anything else. Right now our focus is bringing our daughter home. Everything else will work itself out."

Precious knew Nico was a hundred percent right and that's why she held off on having her lawyer file the annulment papers. She didn't want to add unnecessary stress to an already fragile situation. There would be plenty of time for them to move forward with ending their marriage, but only after Aaliyah was safe and back home Precious decided.

Aaliyah was in the back room rumbling through drawers when she thought she heard a door open. At first she ignored it because Arnez hadn't been gone that long and she knew he couldn't be back already. So Aaliyah continued on her mission to find anything that might assist in her escape. While struggling to open a drawer that seemed to be jammed, she heard the noise again. But this time Aaliyah was positive her mind wasn't playing tricks on her. Arnez was back and she didn't want him to catch her snooping.

Trying to come up with something quick, Aaliyah grabbed a pillow from the bed. She decided she would tell Arnez that her leg was bothering her and needed the pillow to prop her foot. Aaliyah strolled out of the bedroom casually as if she was unaware that he was even back.

"If it isn't my lovely niece. How are you enjoying your accommodations?" Maya had completely caught Aaliyah off guard. It took her a minute to even say a word. "I know you're not speechless," Maya teased.

"I'm just surprised to see you."

"Arnez asked me to come by and keep an eye on you."

"Really, he didn't mention you would be stopping by."

"Why would he? It's not like the two of you are friends."

"Never said we were."

Aaliyah was playing it cool, but there were a few things that had her on high alert. It was no secret she despised Maya, but Aaliyah had no qualms giving credit where credit was due. Although Maya was butt ugly on the inside, you would never know it if you strictly judged her from the outside. She was always on point style-wise. Her hair stayed laid. Face beat, but in a more natural polished way. Clothes: Maya was a label whore, but it was never overdone; kept it classy, understated. And her shoe game was second to none. So her showing up with a baseball cap on, an oversized t-shirt, jeans, and kicks let Aaliyah know to get ready to battle for her life because

Maya came to rumble.

"It's not what you said, but how comfortable you seem. Walking around freely. I even noticed you have a DVD player. Don't tell me you started fuckin' Arnez so you can get some lil' perks during your stay."

"That's just gross, Maya. But why would I expect anything less from the likes of you."

"Careful... careful now. You don't want to upset me. Especially since there is nobody here to protect you."

Aaliyah peeped that while Maya was running her mouth, she kept one hand behind her back. She was positive it was a weapon. *Did this heifa come to kill me? I'm no fan of Arnez, but if and when he wanted me dead, I highly doubt he would send Maya to do the deed; he would kill me himself. So either Maya came just to work my nerves or she's decided on her own that she wants me dead. Whatever it is, I can't take any chances with this trigger-happy nut,* Aaliyah thought to herself.

"You're right but... Ohmigoodness!" Aaliyah jumped around as if frightened. "Is that a rat!" she screamed.

"Where?!" Maya shrieked quickly looking around.

"Over there!" Aaliyah pointed in the direction right behind where Maya was standing.

When Maya turned to look, Aaliyah used the only weapon she had available... the pillow. She lunged towards Maya with the pillow, smashing it over her face. Maya tumbled back hitting the wall and the keys in her pocket fell out. Aaliyah glanced around looking to see if there was anything within reach she could use to slam over Maya's head, but Arnez had the place damn near child-proof to the max. He made sure there was nothing Aaliyah could use as a weapon. The only thing that could do a tad bit of damage was the DVD player. But it was on the other side of the room and Aaliyah knew that would give Maya way too much time to strike back. Instead, Aaliyah had to make use of what she had readily available, her bare feet and hands. She ran up on Maya as she tried to stand up and began stomping her. She could see Maya was reaching for something and figured it had to be a gun, but Aaliyah couldn't get to it.

Instead, she reached down to slam Maya's head on the hardwood floor, but she couldn't get a grip because the baseball cap she was wearing got in her way. When Aaliyah was finally able to knock Maya's cap off and latch onto her hair, Maya took her knee and jammed it into Aaliyah's stomach.

The pain was excruciating and Aaliyah wanted to bend over and hold her stomach, but she was well aware she was battling for her life. One wrong move and it could mean death so she fought through the pain. Aaliyah still had a grip on Maya's hair, so she held it as tightly as possible, lifting her head forward before giving two hard slams. That seemed to put Maya in a semi-daze, which gave Aaliyah a small window of opportunity to reach for her keys and make an exit.

Aaliyah sprinted towards the door holding the keys tightly. She frantically began trying to unlock the door, but there were multiple keys on the chain. In the background, she could hear Maya struggling to get up.

"Come on, which key is it," she mumbled in frustration as none of them were working. It wasn't until Aaliyah got to the very last one that the door finally opened. To her despair, after she opened the first door, there was another one she had to get through in order to reach freedom. Not only that, the door had three different locks. Aaliyah began the process all over again, but this time it wasn't as tedious. The first two locks were opened with ease, but while unlocking the third lock she could hear Maya coming down the hall.

"Fuck!" she snapped in a low tone. As Aaliyah heard Maya get closer, she remained still and moved to the side out of her view. When Maya got right up on the door, Aaliyah swung it back as hard as she could hitting Maya in the head and knocking her out cold. Aaliyah heard her hit the floor and was tempted to swing the door back open and try to get Maya's gun, but she decided making it out while she had a chance was her best option.

"Please don't let there be another door," Aaliyah said out loud after opening the last lock. When the warm night air hit her face she relished the idea of finally being free after what felt like years of being in prison. She wanted to drop to her knees and thank God for letting her escape, but knew Maya could be running up behind her at any minute, so she kept her eyes on the prize. Aaliyah ran up the stairs and wouldn't stop running until she made it back home to her family.

Chapter Sixteen

Do Or Die

"You seem excited about spending the summer with your mom," Supreme commented to Xavier as their flight was preparing to land at LaGuardia Airport.

"I am. When she came to visit for that week, I realized how much I missed being around her. I really do have a pretty cool mom." Xavier grinned. "You're not so bad either, Dad." He laughed.

"Yeah, you better make sure you clean that

up. Don't forget who got you that new truck for your high school graduation," Supreme reminded his son in a joking way.

"I know. That was the best gift. My friends are still begging me to let them drive it. The graduation was unbelievable. Mom was there, my grandparents, and even Grandpa Quentin. It would've been perfect if Aaliyah had showed up. I still can't believe she wasn't able to make it," Xavier said putting his head down.

"I know you were disappointed. Aaliyah wanted to be there, but she got stuck in Mexico."

"She could've at least called me."

Supreme hated to hear the disappointment in Xavier's voice, but there was nothing he could do about it right now. After careful consideration, he and Precious decided it was best not to let Xavier know that his sister was missing. They wanted to wait until they had no choice, but to tell him what was going on. In the meantime, they were doing everything within their power to bring her home alive.

"Listen son, know your sister loves you. Don't think about the negative just hold on to that. I also want you to do something for me."

"What is it, dad?" Xavier looked up at his father wondering what could he possibly want from him."

"You're about to be eighteen soon. I've seen you grow into a remarkable young man. I couldn't have asked for a more incredible son."

"Thank you, Dad. I've looked up to you ever since I can remember and to hear you say that makes me feel good about myself."

"You should, Xavier. You're an exceptional young man. That's why I'm counting on you to look after your mother while you're staying with her during the summer. You have to protect her at all times. Your mother is one of the smartest and strongest women I've ever met, but even she needs someone to watch over her. Don't tell her I said that though."

"I won't. But don't worry. I'll take care of Mom... I promise."

"I'm counting on you." Supreme felt confident his son could handle his request. Mainly because since he was a little boy, Supreme had entrenched all the tools Xavier needed to do so. He not only had the intelligence and book smarts to be anything he wanted to be, but Supreme made sure his son had the street savvy and killer instinct to protect himself and the ones he loves.

"Good because I won't let you down. Although I must admit, it would be nice if you were here to also watch over her. I never gave up wanting to see you and Mom back together," Xaviar admitted, staring out the window as the plan landed.

That was the first time Supreme had ever heard his son say that. Aaliyah was always vocal about wanting her parents together, but Supreme figured that was because all the way up until her teenage years they were husband and wife. Xavier, on the other hand, didn't have that stable two-parent household. While their son was still young, the cracks were beginning to show in the marriage. Supreme and Precious tried to somewhat mask their marital problems, but kids are smart and Xavier soon began to realize that he wasn't living in a happy household. That was one of Supreme's biggest regrets that he wasn't able to give his only son the family stability he craved.

When Aaliyah reached the top of the last step, the smile that was creeping across her face melted into a crushing frown.

"Where the hell do you think you going and how the fuck did yo' sneaky ass even get out!" Arnez barked. He grabbed Aaliyah by her arms and held them behind her back. "Let me pull this gun out so you'll think twice before doing anything else stupid," he warned.

"I didn't do anything stupid! Maya came over here and tried to kill me," Aaliyah blurted.

"What! Don't be making shit up lil' girl," Arnez snarled, gripping Aaliyah's arm tighter.

"Stop callin' me lil' girl," Aaliyah popped as she tried in vain to pull away from his grasp. "How the fuck do you think I was able to get out of that dump? Surely I didn't crawl out the fuckin' window since you got everything barred up like the Florence Supermax Prison," she hissed sarcastically.

"Where is Maya at now?"

"Don't know." Aaliyah shrugged.

When they reached the bottom of the stairs and got through both doors, Maya was beginning to come out of her daze. She wobbled her head trying to focus.

"You! You did this to me! I'ma kill you... you fuckin' bitch!" Maya raged pulling out her gun. She was still off balance due to that knot on her forehead, but it didn't stop her from trying to bust one off.

"Not so fast," Arnez growled snatching the gun out of Maya's hand.

"I told you her crazy ass was tryna kill me," Aaliyah smacked.

"Ain't no trying! I am gonna kill you!" Maya jumped up quick to her feet.

"I guess you feeling better," Aaliyah mocked, finding it funny that Maya was breaking bad with a golf ball-sized lump on the front of her head.

"Oooh, I can't wait to get my hands on you!" Maya charged towards Aaliyah, but Arnez stepped between the two women swiftly. "Move out the fuckin' way." Maya was fuming, swinging her arms wildly.

"Yo, calm the fuck down. Now, Maya." From the bass in his voice, the ladies knew Arnez was done playing with both of them. He was the one holding both the guns, so the women figured it was best to at least try and act like they had some damn sense.

Maya was huffing and puffing like a wild woman, but she stood back not making another move. "Why did you stop me from killing her?" Maya asked between her heavy breathing.

"Because I never gave you the okay to kill Aaliyah."

"I was doing us both a favor. She's dead weight. What are we keeping her alive for... we don't need her."

"I'll decide when we don't need her anymore, but until then she stays alive. Do you understand me?" Maya didn't say a word, but she seemed to be on the verge of hyperventilating. Arnez yanked Maya's arm, pulling her right up to his face. "Do you understand me?"

"Yes," Maya seethed through clenched teeth.

"Good, now you can go."

"You want me to leave?"

"Yes. It's best you go."

"I'm the reason that all this shit is working out for you and now you wanna dismiss me... the nerve of you."

Arnez could see that Maya was on the verge of a complete meltdown and he couldn't afford that. She was already impulsive and Arnez didn't need Maya's behavior becoming even more erratic.

"Maya, I'm not dismissing you. You know how important you are to this operation and me. I wanted you to leave because you're clearly upset and staying here isn't going to make it any better."

"Fine. But let's make one thing clear. It's not if Aaliyah is going to die, it's when. You can either kill her or I will. Make up your mind because I want it done soon."

Maya stormed out leaving no doubt she meant every word she said. Aaliyah glanced over at Arnez and wondered what he was thinking. She didn't know what was scarier. Knowing Maya was determined for her to die or that Arnez held her life in his hands.

Chapter Seventeen

Watching You

"Make sure you call and let me know how things go with Darien," Genesis said as him and Nico wrapped up their business before he left to catch his flight.

"I will. If all goes as planned I should only be in Miami for a couple of days. Any word on Gomez Vargas?"

"As a matter of fact we do have a lead. This Vargas guy has a lounge in Queens. The guy, Bobbie, who's mentioned in those papers we looked through is supposed to work at that lounge. Hopefully, he's still working there. Lorenzo and I are going tomorrow to see what we can find out."

"Damn, I wanna be there for that."

"We'll handle it, Nico. You go take care of Darien Blaze. With this bullshit going on, business has already taken a hit. We can't start letting people who buy our product think they can fuck us over and we won't retaliate."

"Genesis, I'm with you. Remember, it was my idea to teach that foul motherfucker a lesson. I would just prefer to be with you and Lorenzo tomorrow, but I know you'll handle it."

"We will and if I find out any information about Aaliyah, you'll be the first phone call I make. You have my word on that."

"Thank you, man. Let me go so I can catch this flight. Talk to you soon."

After Nico left, Genesis glanced down at his watch and saw the time. "Shit! I was supposed to be at Skylar's place an hour ago." Genesis looked around for his phone. While sending Skylar a text message he heard a knock. *That must be Nico,* he thought as he went to get the door. "You keep coming back you won't ever make that flight," Genesis joked as he was opening the door.

"He'll make the flight. I saw Nico leaving as I

was coming in. How are you?"

"T-Roc, what are you doing here? Come in. It's good to see you, but when we spoke the other day, you didn't mention you would be in town."

"It's good to see you, too. Yeah, I knew I was coming, but I didn't realize it would be this soon."

"So what, you here handling some business?"

"You can call it that. I'll be living here for at least the next year."

"We'll be neighbors again. Welcome back." Genesis smiled.

"Thanks."

"You don't sound excited about the move."

"You know they recently let Chantal out of the psychiatric hospital. I thought the attorney would be able to get it where she could serve out her probation in LA, but that didn't work out."

"Sway was killed here and that's where Chantal was charged with his murder."

"Yeah, and the mental hospital she's been at is in New York. They want her to continue to see the same doctor for her outpatient treatment."

"That makes sense. How is Chantal doing?"

"She seems to be getting better. I'm more concerned about Justina. She's been having a hard time ever since that whole Sway ordeal, but the last few months I've been noticing a lot of improvement. It's like overnight she came out of her shell and found a reason to live again. Now I'm worried us coming back to New York where everything went down might spark a setback."

"Justina has been through a lot and all you can do is be there for her, T-Roc. Kids don't come with a manual, so you do the best you can."

"You should know. You're handling this Amir situation with the same calmness and finesse you do with everything else."

"I've learned when you're surrounded by pandemonium, cool heads will prevail. Amir has lost his girlfriend to a horrendous murder and he's being charged with it. If I don't stay calm, this shit will blow up in his face. Then Aaliyah's missing and I know he's taking that hard. We all are." Genesis sighed.

"Aaliyah's missing... what happened?"

"Remember I mentioned that we were having some problems with business."

"Yeah, I remember."

"I downplayed how serious it is. We've taken some major hits and now Aaliyah has become a target. If we don't get this situation under control soon, I'm afraid Amir will end up spending the rest of his life behind bars for a murder he didn't commit and Aaliyah will end up dead."

"I can't believe you're finally here," Precious beamed hugging Xavier. "Go take a look at your room. I redid it for you. I put everything in there that I believed my wonderful teenage son would love."

"Thanks, Mom!" Xavier grinned, taking his luggage and heading towards the hallway.

"Don't spend this entire summer spoiling our son or he won't wanna head off to college when it's time," Supreme scoffed.

"Would that be so bad? It's not like Xavier can't be successful without college... look at his father."

"Xavier wants to attend college. He wants to be an attorney."

"Are you serious? I had no idea. Wow, I feel like a loser parent."

"Don't. He only started talking about it recently."

"That makes me feel better. But for the record, I was only joking about college. You know how important I think education is. I even went back to school myself."

"I remember. I was so proud of you when you made that decision."

"I was proud of myself, too. I always hoped Aaliyah would decide to attend college. I was so disappointed when she ran off to Miami and became a bartender." Precious gasped. "But now, I would give anything to know she was alive, pouring drinks somewhere. It doesn't matter what your kids do as long as they're happy, healthy, and safe."

"Baby, please don't cry," Supreme said, pulling Precious in close. "We will find Aaliyah alive." He stroked her hair and the aroma of Precious' seductive perfume made Supreme move in closer. He didn't want to admit it to himself, but he was still very drawn to his ex-wife.

"In my heart I believe that too, but I can't lie, I'm scared. With each day that passes, I feel my faith slipping away."

"Don't. Keep the faith. Our daughter is coming home." Supreme wanted to lean over and kiss Precious, but fought against it. "I need to go."

"So soon? I thought you would stay for a little while. Maybe the three of us could go out to lunch."

"I have something really important I need to do, but maybe if you're not busy the three of us can have dinner."

"I would love that and I think Xavier would too." Precious didn't even try to contain her excitement.

"Then I'll see the two of you later on. Tell Xavier I'll see him when I get back."

"I will." Precious felt like she was going to have a permanent smile plastered across her face while waving goodbye to Supreme. For the first time since regaining her memory, she had hope that he was letting her back in. *Maybe we can be a family again,* Precious thought as her heart yearned for that more than anything.

Amir had to do a double take when he saw a familiar face going into a boutique on Lexington Avenue. He quickly headed in that direction to make sure his mind wasn't playing tricks on him. When he entered the store, his eyes scanned the place.

"Sir, can I help you?" a sales clerk asked.

"No, I'm good," Amir said heading to the back of the store. "Justina, is that you?" he questioned turning her around.

"Amir, hi. This is the last place I expected to run into you."

"I was walking down the street and for a minute I wasn't sure if I was seeing things. You really look fantastic," Amir said noticing the golden blond highlights in her hair. To compliment her new hair color, Justina was wearing some distressed boyfriend jeans, a white-cropped sequin shirt, and some Christian Louboutin Kristali Laser Cut pumps. It was a completely different style for her, bold and sexy, not Justina's usual, unpretentious choices in fashion.

"Thank you." Justina lowered her head as if she was uncomfortable by Amir's compliment.

"You're welcome. I can't believe you're in New York and you didn't call me."

"I was planning to, but I know you have a lot going on."

"I guess that means you heard about Latreese. But who hasn't, it's been in the paper and the news. You still could've called me. We're supposed to be friends."

"You're right, I should've called."

"How long are you going to be in New York?"

"My mom has to do her probation here so we'll be calling New York home for a long time."

"Even though it might not be under the best circumstances, I'm glad you're here. I need a friend right now."

"What about Aaliyah? You all have always been close."

"True, but Aaliyah has been out of town for

awhile and I'm not sure when she's coming back."
Amir didn't think this was the right time to tell
Justina that someone had taken Aaliyah, so he
told her what he considered to be an innocent lie.

"I see. Well listen, it was good seeing you,
but I need to go."

"But you haven't even finished shopping."

"I wasn't planning on buying anything; I was
buying time. I have to go meet my dad."

"Do you have to rush off so soon? There's
this restaurant on the corner that has the best
shrimp and lobster. I know how much you love
seafood. We can have a drink and catch up. It'll
be good to hear what you've been up to. It might
even take my mind off all the madness going on
in my life."

"Maybe another time. I really have to go,"
Justina said rushing off.

"Justina wait!" Amir called out, but she
continued out the door not looking back. *That
was weird. I wonder why Justina ran off like that,*
Amir wondered, running out the store trying to
catch up to her. When he got outside, Amir looked
around, but she was gone.

From across the street, Gomez Vargas was
sitting in his car watching everything unfold.
He had started following Amir a week ago. After
reading the article in the paper, he made it a

mission to find out everything he could about the man being accused of killing Kendra. It took Gomez a minute to track him down, but once he did, he spent all his free time tracking Amir's every move.

"What you think just happened?" Bennie, Gomez's right hand man, asked from the passenger seat.

"If I had to guess, I would say he came rushing out looking for that pretty young thing we just saw get in a cab."

"Sounds about right. You think he has a new girlfriend already?"

"Who knows. A young, rich, good-looking guy like that more than likely has several girlfriends. That's probably why he had no problem killing Kendra."

"So you really convinced he did it?"

"Positive."

"But why? A rich guy like that who seems to have everything, why would he throw it all away?"

"It's always the privileged fucks who think they can get away with anything. He might've found out she had been lying to him about being some college girl named Latreese. When he discovered she was actually a ran-through prostitute named Kendra Watkins, he flipped out and killed her, 'cause he felt embarrassed and stupid."

"I could see that." Bennie nodded his head in agreement."

"You know his father is supposed to be some major player in the game. I'm sure Amir was thinking his daddy will help him get away with murder too."

"Gomez, you know I'm down for whatever you wanna do, but why do you even care? I figured you wiped your hands of Kendra after you sold her to that other broad."

"Because Kendra belonged to me. I bought and paid for her... she didn't cost me much, but she made me a lot of money. Kendra was a solid moneymaker. It was my choice to sell her and didn't no one have the right to kill her, but me. Not some lil' rich kid punk."

"I feel you. Have you been able to get in touch with the broad you sold her to yet?"

"Nope. I'm beginning to feel like she's ignoring my calls. I want to find out how Kendra went from working for her to being the girlfriend of this Amir character. She has some explaining to do and I'ma get my answers. But for now, I'm keeping my eyes on him," Gomez said driving off when he saw Amir was back on the move.

Chapter Eighteen

Live From The Gutter

When Supreme arrived at the address he had in his phone he wasn't expecting to find an abandoned warehouse. But his source was adamant this was the correct location and he had never been wrong in the past. He went around to the back and the door was unlocked.

The place was completely empty and unnervingly quiet. Anyone else might've been worried and felt like they were entering into a deathtrap, but not Supreme. He was well aware what he was walking into and he came prepared.

"If it isn't the legendary Xavier Mills aka Supreme."

"Death looks good on you, Arnez. I thought I was gonna find you in a gutter somewhere. I guess this place is close enough." Arnez was doing a good job hiding it, but Supreme could tell he was the last person Arnez was expecting to see.

"I'm impressed. How did you find me?"

"I still hold a lot of weight in these streets. There aren't too many people I can't find... except for one."

"And who would that be?"

"My daughter, Aaliyah."

"I'm sorry to hear that. No one should be without their child. I hope you find her."

"I agree and I don't plan on being without her for very long."

"That's good to hear. So what brings you all the way to Staten Island? This is a long way from the luxury of Beverly Hills."

"We go way back, Arnez."

"Yes, we do. When I discovered you in Queens as a young street rapper, I knew you had what it took to go far, but never in my wildest dreams did I think you would go as far as you did. I mean you went all the way." Arnez chuckled. "But you know what I really respect about you, Supreme."

"What's that?"

"With all the wealth, fame and notoriety, the streets still love you. You can go to any hood right now in any borough and you have they heart. Not too many rappers that made it to your level can say that. I personally witnessed your rise to superstardom. I feel like I'ma part of history since I was there from the beginning," Arnez said proudly.

"It's because of that history we share that I'm giving you one opportunity."

"And what opportunity is that?"

"To keep living. When it got back to me that you might be alive, I said to myself no way. Why would Arnez be alive and not let me know, unless of course it wasn't beneficial to your plans. I mean, I'm well aware you have some unfinished business and I'm cool with that as long as it has nothing to do with my family or me. I would kill for mine and die too. But since we go way back you already know that about me," Supreme said, easing his way closer towards Arnez.

"I do."

"That's why I'm certain that if you knew anything about what happened to my daughter you would tell me."

"I would."

"That's good, we're on the same page. Here's the thing. I want my daughter home. Precious is trying desperately to keep it together, but inside she's crumbling. No mother should have to go through that so I need to make this right. Do you wanna help me make this right, Arnez?"

"Of course I do."

"Wonderful. We're making progress." Supreme smirked, rubbing his hands together. "I need as many people as possible helping me with this. "I've already obtained the services of some extremely efficient and ruthless killers to assist me. They're simply waiting for me to press go. But before the bloodshed starts, I wanna give whoever is responsible for taking my daughter an opportunity to rectify their fuckup."

"I see. That's very generous of you."

"I think so too, but my generosity has an expiration date that's fast approaching. You've already agreed to help me though so I'm feeling more optimistic."

"I'll definitely help you in any way I can."

Supreme was now eye to eye with Arnez. They were so close they could hear each other breathing. "You better help me because if I don't get my daughter back soon, death will seem like a gift to you. Are we clear?"

"Perfectly clear."

"Then I'm done here."

Arnez's right eye began twitching from staring so hard at Supreme as he was leaving. He kept his anger on simmer although Arnez was ready to explode. His fury wasn't aimed at Supreme though. Arnez placed the blame squarely on Maya for his current predicament and now it was time for her to go.

"You can come out now," Arnez said, peeping through a tiny window as Supreme drove away.

"That was the one and only Supreme. I'm a fan of his, but this didn't seem like the right time to introduce myself," Emory said coming out of hiding. "It's a good thing you saw him pull up or he would've caught us together. We don't need anyone knowing our business affiliation."

"Supreme showing up here isn't good at all."

"I agree, but what I found the most interesting was him questioning you about Aaliyah. Tell me you don't have anything to do with her disappearance."

"I don't."

"Arnez, if you did something to that girl, I'll have to cut my ties with you right now. My brother finds out I was dealing with you and you took Aaliyah he will wanna kill me," Emory barked pointing his finger at his chest. "But the

difference is, he'll let me live, but he will kill you."
Emory then pointed that same finger at Arnez.
"I can't have no parts of that. I'm not losing my
brother over no dumb shit."

"Calm the fuck down. I told you I don't have
Aaliyah!" Arnez barked back, feeling the walls
closing in on him.

"Dale is in New York right now searching for
answers. He want his woman back and whoever
has her is a dead man. Is that dead man gon' be
you?" Emory demanded to know.

"How many times do I have to tell you that I
do not have Aaliyah?"

"Then why did Supreme sound so sure that
you did?"

"He figures I might know something and
I can help. The threats was Supreme's way
of motivating me to step forward if I do hear
anything, that's all." Arnez was trying his best to
sell his story, but he could see Emory wasn't sold.

"I need to get back to the hotel. Dale is
waiting for me."

"You'll be set when it's time for us to make
our next move?"

"I'll be in touch." That was the only answer
Emory was willing to give Arnez.

"Dammit!" Arnez shouted, kicking over the
chair once he was alone. "Maya, I'm not gonna let

you ruin this for me." He couldn't contain his outrage. He was ready to tear down the walls in the warehouse. Arnez had to devise a new strategy and fast or else his plans would blow up in his face.

Genesis and Lorenzo sat in the back of the black tinted SUV observing the comings and goings of people in Gomez's lounge. It was early, but there was a steady amount of traffic flowing through the doors.

"You ready to go inside?" Lorenzo asked Genesis.

"Yep, let's go."

"Are you sure you don't want us to come in?" Brice asked Lorenzo and Genesis.

"No, you and Sean stay out here. There's already three of our security inside. Across the street in the black van is Damon and them. So if shit start looking shaky you know what to do," Genesis said before him and Lorenzo got out the truck.

"There's not too much going on in here," Lorenzo commented when they entered inside the rather small lounge. It did have an intimate feel where once you were inside you wouldn't mind staying for a while.

"Feel free to sit where you like unless you want to get a table, but you'll have to get bottle service," the hostess said when she noticed they were standing around.

"We'll take a table," Genesis said.

The hostess smiled before showing them to a table right in the center of the lounge. "Your waitress will be over to take your order in a moment."

"I like where we're sitting. We have a clear view of everyone."

"Me too. Did you notice our security over in the corner." Genesis nodded his head in the area they were standing.

"It's good to know everyone is in position incase a problem arises. But where is this Bobbie guy... do you think he was the one working the door when we first came in?"

"It's a good chance. When our waitress gets here, I'll ask her without raising any suspicions. I think this woman coming in our direction would be her," Genesis said. "Let's see if she can point us in the right direction."

"What can I get you gentlemen a bottle of?" The waitress gave both of them a seductive smile, but her eyes lingered on Lorenzo for an extended period of time and it didn't go unnoticed. After

Genesis ordered a bottle of champagne for the table he signaled Lorenzo to start asking the question since it was obvious the waitress was flirting with him.

"Sorry, I didn't get your name." Lorenzo extended his hand and the waitress gladly took it.

"Juliette."

"Pretty name. So Juliette how long have you been working here?"

"I'm one of the newer girls. Only six months."

"How do you like it?"

"The hours are long, but the tips are good. Every once in awhile I also get to meet some rather intriguing men." Juliette winked at Lorenzo.

"Beautiful young lady like you, I'm sure men are constantly coming at you. Not only customers, but people you work with you too."

"Yeah, all the time."

"What about my man Bobbie. You're exactly his type. Where is he anyway?" Lorenzo questioned, glancing around the lounge as if looking for Bobbie. "Isn't he working tonight?"

"Bobbie?" Juliette asked as if puzzled. "The only Bobbie I know that works here is the bartender," Juliette turned her head towards the bar. "And she's definitely no he."

"Maybe the Bobbie I'm talking about quit before you started working here."

"Maybe so. If he did, that Bobbie," Juliette pointed to the bartender, "would definitely know. She's been working here for years."

"Got you. I'll have to ask her because I thought for sure my man Bobbie was still working here. Maybe the bartender can tell me when he quit."

"I'm sure she can, but if you need any other type of assistance I'll be happy to help." Juliette smiled, stroking Lorenzo's hand. "I'll go get the champagne and be right back."

"That Juliette was coming on strong." Genesis laughed.

"Sure was. Too bad for her I'm already taken."

"But lucky for us she was helpful. Here we were looking for a man and Bobbie is a female."

"That's why you should never assume. But the bartender has to be the Bobbie we're looking for. While you go talk to her, I'ma see if I can get some more information about Gomez Vargas from Juliette," Lorenzo said.

When Genesis got to the bar, Bobbie was pouring a customer a drink. There was only one other person sitting down so Genesis took a seat at the end stool. After waiting a few minutes, the bartender eventually made her way to him.

"What can I get you to drink?"

Genesis had no interest in pretending he wanted anything other than information. He placed a hundred dollar bill on top of the bar. "What will this get me?"

"Depends on what you want."

Genesis then put another hundred dollar bill on top of the bar. "A few weeks ago you spoke to a private investigator."

"And?" she said wiping down the bar as to appear she was doing her job in case anyone was watching her.

"I need some more information."

"I told that man everything I know. I don't see how I can help you."

"Let me ask the questions and decide. Either way you still get paid," Genesis said adding another one hundred dollar bill.

Bobbie poured Genesis a drink and discreetly scanned the lounge. She had no intentions of losing out on some easy money or getting caught doing so. She placed a drink down in front of Genesis and he took that as an indication that she was ready to talk.

"You said that you heard your boss Gomez Vargas mention a man by the name of Arnez."

"Yes, I did."

"In what context?"

"Are you asking why did Gomez mention Arnez to me?"

"Yes."

"He didn't," Bobbie said.

"I'm not following you. If Gomez didn't mention Arnez to you then how did you hear him say the name?"

"I overheard him having a conversation with someone else and he mentioned Arnez. This was a couple years ago."

"Who was he having the conversation with?"

"I don't know her name, but she used to come in here sometimes. She did business with Gomez."

"Have you seen her in here recently?"

"No. I haven't seen her since around that time."

"How can you be so sure that you heard them mention Arnez when it was so long ago?' Genesis was curious to know.

"Gomez used to have this really sweet girl work for him named Kendra. I would try to look out for her whenever I could. I liked her a lot. So if I heard her name being mentioned, I would pay close attention.

"Got you," Genesis nodded. "So what did you hear?"

"He was talking to that woman that he did business with, she told Gomez she wanted to buy Kendra from him. He laughed and said was Kendra going to be a gift for her friend Arnez who just came back from the dead. I thought it was some inside joke between the two of them. The woman said no that she wanted Kendra for another man."

"This woman Kendra, does she still work for Gomez?"

"No, unfortunately she's dead," Bobbie said sadly.

"Dead... did Gomez have something to do with that?"

"No, some other man was arrested for her murder. I think it was her boyfriend. I saw it in the paper recently. It's really sad because Kendra was young and had a lot of potential. It's too bad she ever had to deal with the likes of Gomez."

Genesis learned a long time ago not to believe in coincidences. It struck him as odd that this woman Kendra and Amir's girlfriend Latreese were killed recently and their boyfriends were both being accused of the murder. It was possible, but highly unlikely.

"This Kendra woman. Do you know her last name?"

"Watkins. Her name was Kendra Watkins."

"You said she worked for Gomez. What did she do?"

Bobbie seemed to be reluctant to answer Genesis. He saw her hesitation so he pulled out another hundred dollar bill. The stack of money was growing steadily. She remained on mute so Genesis kept adding more.

"It's not about you adding more money," Bobbie finally said. "

"Then what?" Genesis questioned with a raised eyebrow.

"I was a lot older than Kendra so we didn't hang out together. Gomez kept her on a short leash anyway. But I cared about her. She was a good girl that was caught up in the wrong life. I don't want to seem like I'm talking badly of her or for you to pass judgment."

"Lady, I'm in no position to pass judgment on anybody... so please continue."

— "She was a prostitute and Gomez was her pimp."

Genesis didn't even want to consider that Kendra Watkins and Latreese were one in the same, but his gut was telling him they were. If so, Amir's belief that he was set up for Latreese's murder made a lot of sense. She had to be connected to Arnez, but he didn't know how. Genesis figured the woman who was doing business with Gomez had to be the missing link. If he was able to speak to this mystery woman, Genesis knew he would get all the answers he needed and he was determined to find her.

Chapter Nineteen

I'm Coming Home

"You know what to say right?" Arnez said handing Aaliyah the cell.

"I'm not calling her." Aaliyah pushed the phone away.

"Don't you want your mother to know that you're okay?"

"Not if I'm going to end up dead anyway. Why would I put my mother through that? Calling her, letting her hear my voice, giving her hope that she'll see me again, only to end up dead. I rather her start mourning for me now then have to mourn later."

"Why do you have to make shit so complicated?" He grumbled. "Glad I never had kids 'cause a child like you would've drove me crazy.

Aaliyah gave him no reaction. She remained seated on the couch using the nail filer Arnez had given her. After filing down her middle finger she stuck it out as if admiring her work. She then applied a clear top coat of polish and blew on her nails so they would dry faster.

With her fuck you attitude turned all the way up, if Arnez didn't know better he would've sworn that Aaliyah knew Supreme had paid him a visit and now he was working overtime to save his own ass. He was more than ready to see her go. Arnez had planned out how he would do it, but not surprisingly Aaliyah was not cooperating,

"I have no intention of killing of you," Arnez confessed.

"Whatever. You're only saying that because you want me to call my mother. It ain't gonna happen."

"I swear. I plan on letting you go in a week. I didn't want to tell you because I didn't want you stressing me about it every day. But I am letting you go."

"Really? You sounding awfully persuasive."

"'Cause it's the truth."

"When and why did you make this decision?"

"See, this is the exact reason I didn't wanna tell you shit. Instead of you being happy, staying quiet, and playing yo' position, you wanna ask me twenty million questions."

"I have a right to know. I'm not calling my mother until I'm convinced this is real."

"I never had any intention of killing you. All I was trying to do was protect you." Arnez was well aware this would be a hard sell. It was one of the main reasons he wasn't ready to disclose the information to Aaliyah. He wanted more time to work out the kinks in his story, but she wasn't leaving him a choice so he had to wing it.

"Protect me? Boy, try again." Aaliyah rolled her eyes.

"It's the truth. I didn't want to tell you until I was able to connect all the dots and I'm close to being able to do that."

"You still haven't told me who you are protecting me from."

"Maya."

Aaliyah burst out laughing. "You can't be serious. If you hadn't put that gun to my head, Maya would be dead right now. So I didn't need your protection."

"I couldn't let you kill Maya because I didn't know who she was working with to bring down your family and I still don't but I'm close to finding out."

"Aren't you the person who is working with Maya to bring my family down?"

"I needed it to appear that way so Maya would trust me. Maya and I were involved in an intimate relationship. During some pillow talk she mentioned she hated her family and was working with someone to destroy them and also make a lot of money. She asked me did I want in on it because she was well aware of my history with Genesis. I told her I would. It was only so I could find who she was working with and put a stop to it. But Maya has been playing it very close to the vest when it comes to her partner."

"This all sounds very intriguing. The only problem is why would you give a fuck about helping my family?"

"Because of your father... Supreme."

"You know my father?"

"Yes, very well. I was the one who gave him his start in music. To this day, I have a great deal of respect for your father."

"Wow, this is getting stranger and stranger. If you know my father, then why didn't you tell him you have me?"

"Aaliyah, don't you understand? You and your family are in danger until I know who Maya is working with. If I were to go to Supreme or your family, Maya would know it came from me. They could contain her, but whoever Maya's partner is would remain free to cause havoc on your family. It's best that I keep Supreme in the dark."

"This all seems a tad bizarre."

"That's understandable, but think about it. When Maya came here to kill you, I didn't let her. I've kept Maya as far away from you as possible. If I wasn't loyal to Supreme, it wouldn't matter to me whether you lived or died."

"So you're letting me... why not today? Why do you have to wait a week?"

"Because by then I'll know who Maya is teamed up with and I can tell your family. At that point, they'll know who the enemy is and how to strike back. But I know your family must be worried about you, especially your mother. That's why I want you to call her. Your mother needs to know you're coming home."

Aaliyah wasn't completely sold on Arnez's 'I'm your savior' story, but she did believe he was going to let her live and set her free. For now that was enough to make her a little bit more cooperative.

"Hand me the phone."

"Can I trust you to stick to what we discussed?" Arnez asked.

"Yes. I'll keep it short and sweet. Now hand me the phone before I change my mind."

Arnez placed the cell in her hand. He wasn't certain he made Aaliyah a believer, but he thought his story was plausible enough to raise reasonable doubt. That would have to suffice for now because Arnez had a week to turn this around. He would have to put a large chunk of his plans on hold to focus on not only getting rid of Maya, but having all evidence of guilt point solely in her direction.

"Skylar, this apartment is stunning. But I wouldn't expect anything less from Genesis." Precious smiled.

"Thank you. I love it too. Genesis truly is amazing," Skylar said putting down the glass of wine she was drinking. "I know you have to be leaving soon so let me show you around before you go."

"Finally. I didn't want to be rude and start showing myself around." Precious laughed.

"Follow me." Skylar took the last few sips of her drink and began showing Precious around.

Precious couldn't help but be awestruck with the impressive penthouse. The classically laid out floorplan of the elegant residence was spacious, especially for New York City. Then there was the unparalleled craftsmanship and design of limestone mantels, antique chandelier and sconces with exquisite architectural detailing including intricate moldings, soaring arches, 14 to 20 foot ceilings, and columns.

"This is the last stop which as you can see is my son's bedroom."

"Very cute indeed. Seems like yesterday my son Xavier had a bedroom similar to this. Makes you feel like you're at a toy store. Now he's about to go to college."

"I know what you mean. Time flies. Seems like yesterday I was pregnant, now my lil' man is having meaningful conversations with me. I miss his company already."

"Where is he?" Precious questioned.

"Yesterday he went back to California to stay with my mom. During the summer he spends a great deal of time with her, which she loves and so does he. Now that we're living in New York I can't just drive to mom's house to go see him whenever I want. But he loves his grandma so I'll have to keep myself busy until he gets back."

"Both Aaliyah and Xavier were very close to Supreme's parents at that age. I know you miss him, but I'm sure Genesis will be more than happy to keep you company while your son is gone."

"I've been living here for weeks now, but Genesis has pretty much been MIA. I know he has a lot going on, especially with Amir having been arrested."

"He does, but I know it must be hard being in a new city and the person you moved here for isn't able to really be around."

"Very hard, but I knew what I was signing up for. Genesis has always been upfront with me. He never painted this idyllic picture perfect life. But the good outweighs the bad and I love him."

"I see. It's written all over your face. Genesis clearly loves you, too. He's let you into his life and has provided a beautiful home for you and your son."

"He really has. Things might be somewhat rocky now, but I know in the end he's worth it."

"I can't argue with that. Genesis is a wonderful man. He's been through a lot in the relationship department, but you make him incredibly happy. I can tell."

"Thank you so much for saying that, Precious. It means a lot since I know you're not one to mince words."

"That is true. I'm not exactly known for my politeness." Both women laughed.

"I know you have to be going so let me grab my purse, freshen up, and we can walk out together. They're some things I need to pick up for the apartment."

"Cool, take your time." Precious was admiring the European antique chandelier in the dining room when she felt her iPhone vibrating. "I wonder who this is," she said seeing unknown across the screen of her phone. "Hello."

"Hi, Mom."

"Aaliyah! How are you... where are you?" Precious' voice was panicked.

"Calm down, Mom. I'm fine. I can't talk long, but I wanted you to know that I was okay and I'll be home in a week."

"Baby, where are you? Are you hurt?"

"I'm not hurt. I'm fine. I'll tell you everything when I get home. I love you. Bye."

"I love...." Before Precious could get the rest of her words out Aaliyah had hung up.

"All ready! Hope I didn't take too long," Skylar said in a bubbly voice. "Precious, is everything okay? You look like you're in a daze."

"I'll tell you about it on the elevator."

By the time the women exited Skylar's apartment building, Precious had dissected her call with Aaliyah twenty different ways during their elevator ride.

"Precious, any of those scenarios might be true, but the most important thing is you heard from Aaliyah and she's okay."

"You're right. Thanks, Skylar," Precious said giving her a hug. "I'll call you later. Maybe we can do dinner or something."

"Sounds great!"

Precious waved bye to Skylar before reaching in her purse to call Supreme. Rushing to her car and simultaneously making a call distracted her so much that Precious almost didn't hear the muffled screams ringing in the air. She turned around and saw two men trying to drag Skylar into a van. Precious raced to her car to retrieve her gun. From the short distance Precious could see that Skylar was doing her best to fight off her attackers, but she was losing the battle.

"Get the fuck away from her!' Precious hollered, firing shots at the men, but trying her best not to hit Skylar in the process.

"Leave me alone!" Skylar begged, trying to squirm her body away from the men. With Precious busting shots and Skylar moving around wildly, one of the men punched her in her face to gain control of the situation.

Another man jumped out the van firing shots back at Precious and shielding the men at the same time. Precious ducked behind a car and could see Skylar's body slump over as the man swung her over his shoulder and tossed her in the van. The gunman let off another round of bullets before taking refuge in the van.

"Stooop!" Precious yelled out in vain as the van sped off with Skylar inside. She tried to get the plate number, but it didn't have any tags. "Fuuuuuck!!" Precious yelled over and over again, dreading her next call.

"Hey, Precious. I'm finishing up a conversation with Lorenzo. Can I call you back in about ten minutes."

"No. Genesis, I need for you to get to Skylar's place ASAP." Her panting was heavy and there was no denying the urgency in her voice.

"I'm on the way."

Precious went back to her car to wait for Genesis. She put her head down on the steering wheel and was flooded with despair. Out of all the people she hated that this was happening to Skylar. She wasn't a part of this criminal world, but was forced into it because she fell in love with the wrong man. Precious knew all too well how cruel the game could be, so it killed her inside to know that the next time she would see Skylar might be in a casket.

Chapter Twenty

Uncovering The Truth

"So, Gomez, what's so urgent that you've been blowing up my phone nonstop?" Maya scoffed, as she read through some of her text messages.

"I don't understand you. We did a lot of business together then after I sold you Kendra, you disappear for a very long time. Then you call me out the blue and say you want to do more business with me. But when I try to reach out to you, I get nothing. That's very disrespectful,"

Gomez complained.

"A lot is going on. I have every intention of doing some new business with you though. I was waiting for my partner to come into town and now he's here. I was thinking tomorrow we could all get together."

"Tomorrow will work. Unlike you, I make time for business associates."

"I'm catching the shade, but Gomez, it isn't necessary. You've made your point."

"Good because I have another point to make."

"Which is..." Maya began tapping her shoe, becoming annoyed with Gomez's whining.

"If I sold Kendra to you, how did she end up dead?"

"I have no idea. I read it in the paper just like you."

"But Kendra was supposed to be working for you."

"And she was. She started seeing that Amir guy behind my back. One day she came to me and said she was in love and wanted out. "

"So you just let her go?" Gomez frowned.

"No, I didn't just let her go," Maya snapped. "She gave me the money back I spent to buy her from you, plus interest. I still wasn't going to let her go, but when I found out who the man was, I washed my hands of it. He has a very powerful father that I didn't want any problems with."

"I see. You might have been afraid, but I'm not. This Amir will pay for killing Kendra."

"Do what you have to do." Maya shrugged. "Was that the urgency... Kendra's murder was the reason you were blowing my phone up like a madman? If so, I must be going now. I have more pressing business to tend to. But I'll be in touch for the meeting tomorrow," Maya said turning to walk away.

"Wait!" Gomez demanded.

"What else is it?" Maya put her arms up, indicating for Gomez to hurry it up.

"Two men came to my lounge the other night asking questions about Arnez."

Maya's back was turned away from Gomez and she was glad he couldn't see her eyes widen with concern. Now this was something she considered urgent, but Maya wanted to play it cool and get all the facts before panicking in fear.

"Really? Why would some men come to your lounge asking questions about Arnez?" Maya was extremely blasé with her approach to the question.

"I'm not sure. But from my understanding, they somehow found out I knew Arnez wasn't dead, but very much alive."

"Interesting."

"Yes, they also wanted to know who was the woman I was doing business with that was involved with Arnez."

"What did you tell them?" It took all of Maya's strength not to gag.

"I haven't told them anything because they haven't had a chance to speak to me yet. But I'm sure the men will be back. They didn't see me, but I saw them when they were leaving and I recognized the men."

"You did... who was it?"

"Genesis, Amir's father. I know this because not only did I dig up all the information I could when I found out Amir killed Kendra, I've also been following him. The other man, I'm not sure who he is. I've seen him before. Do you recognize him?" Gomez showed Maya a picture that was taken of Genesis and Lorenzo when they were outside his lounge.

"No, I don't," Maya lied, knowing the other man was Lorenzo.

"So what should I do, Maya? Should I tell the men that it was you who told me that Arnez was alive?"

"I honestly don't think that would be a good idea, Gomez. If these men have a problem with Arnez and they find out that we're involved that could turn into a problem for me and neither of us want that."

"I figured as much. I have no problem keeping your secret, Maya. But we both know keeping secrets come at a high price. We don't have to discuss that now. As I know you will be answering all my calls from this day forward."

Gomez spoke with a thick Dominican accent and normally Maya found it cute even somewhat sexy, but today it sounded like nails scratching a chalkboard. She had to grin and bare it, but inside she was cringing with disgust.

"Of course. I apologize if you feel I haven't been giving you the respect you deserve. I will make sure that never happens again." She smiled.

"You are a very wise woman, Maya. I will see you tomorrow."

"Yes, I'm looking forward to it."

Gomez gave Maya a smirk like he was taunting her. She waited until he got inside his car before running after him. "Gomez, hold on for a minute," she yelled out waving her hand.

Gomez rolled down his window, "What is it?"

"Where's Bennie, he's not with you?"

"I needed Bennie to keep his eyes on Amir. He's the only one I trust to do that."

"Yes, Bennie has always been very loyal to you," Maya said glancing around the desolate parking lot. "My partner wanted to speak with you briefly before we meet tomorrow. Is that okay with you?"

"Of course. Is he on the phone now?"

"No, let me call him back. I wasn't sure I would be able to catch up to you in time."

"Call him back now. As I told you before, I always make time for my business associates."

"Yes, you do," Maya said reaching in her purse. Maya unloaded two shots to the side of Gomez's head so swiftly; he didn't even realize he was about to die. "Nothing personal Gomez, but you're another headache that I can't afford to have." Maya took one more glance around the parking lot before making a clean escape.

Genesis was sitting on the wrought iron chair on his private terrace when Nico came out. He stood back and observed his friend tightly clutching his cell for a few minutes before making his presence known.

"Do you mind if I sit down?" Nico waited for Genesis to respond, but he simply shook his head no. "Have you heard anything?" Nico asked taking a seat across from Genesis.

"Not yet. They've had her for three days

and nothing. Not a phone call, a ransom note... nothing."

"Don't think the worse, Genesis. I've been where you're at. I was starting to think I would never see Aaliyah again, but Precious spoke to her. She's still alive and if we are to believe what Aaliyah said, she'll be home soon. This could very well be the case with Skylar."

"I want to believe that more than anything. I keep staring at my phone, trying to make it ring and for the person on the other end to tell me what they want in order to let Skylar go. That call hasn't come yet and I'm beginning to think it never will," Genesis admitted somberly.

"Stop thinking like that. Anything is possible. Look at me. After all these years I find out that the child I thought Lisa had aborted is alive and her name is Angel. If I hadn't gone seeking revenge on Darien Blaze, I might've left this earth never knowing about my other daughter. Yes, she's missing and I'm doing everything to find her, but just like I believe Aaliyah is coming home I also believe I will find Angel again. You have to keep that same faith, Genesis. If not, you'll die inside."

"You're right. I have to believe. Good or bad I will get through this. I have to."

"Have you spoken to Amir yet?"

"I did, but I didn't want to tell him what I

found out about Latreese over the phone. He should be here any minute now. His lawyer was able to get permission from the courts to let him handle some business in Philly for me. He texted me a little while ago saying he was on his way over."

"Speaking of Amir, here he comes now," Nico said as he and Genesis both turned towards the terrace entrance.

"Hey Nico, Dad, how you holding up?" Amir said giving his father a hug. Amir hadn't seen his father since Skylar had been kidnapped although they had spoken several times on the phone.

"I'm hanging in there, son. Everything go good in Philly?"

"As well as can be expected. I met with our core customers and they're getting somewhat antsy, but they've promised to remain loyal while we're maneuvering through our difficulties. They appreciated that you sent me down there to speak with them in person."

"I knew they would. Thank you for handling that."

"Thank you for believing that I could handle it. You've been trusting me with more and more responsibilities and that only makes me want to work harder and make you proud."

"I am proud of you, Amir, but there was

something I wanted to talk to you about."

"I'ma leave the two of you alone. I'll be in-side making some phone calls," Nico said excus-ing himself. He was well aware what Genesis was going to discuss with his son and felt it should be dealt with in private between the two of them.

"Dad, what's going on? I mean, Nico excusing himself. He's family. We can discuss anything in front of him."

"Nico knows what I'm about to discuss with you, but he also understands this is going to be difficult for you to hear."

"What could possibly be that difficult for me to hear?"

"How did you meet Latreese?"

"Latreese... what does Latreese have to do with this?"

"Amir, just answer the question."

"I met her at a party."

"What party?"

"The birthday party you and Nico threw for Quentin over a year ago. Why... why are you asking me this?"

"Because Latreese isn't who you thought she was. She changed her name. She was really Kendra Watkins."

"What!" Amir was understandably baffled. "Dad, that has to be a mistake. Why would

Latreese have changed her name?"

"She was a prostitute. She worked for a man named Gomez Vargas."

"Gomez Vargas... why does that name sound so familiar?"

"He's the man that was mentioned in connection with Arnez."

"Are you saying that Latreese was somehow involved with Arnez?"

"Yes, how I don't know."

Amir was pacing the terrace with his arms behind his head. "I was a mark. She used me. The entire time we were together, Latreese was using me."

"Son, calm down. What we need to focus on is finding out who hired Latreese. "

"It had to be Arnez."

"I don't think so."

"Who else could it be? I'm telling you Arnez is behind all of this."

"If Arnez is behind this, he had help. You said you met Latreese at Quentin's birthday party. How would Arnez know about that? That was a private party. Only close friends and family were invited."

"Maya." Amir said without hesitation. "Aaliyah was right. It's been Maya this entire time. We have to find her!" Amir barked, ready to head for the door.

"Amir, wait!" Genesis yelled out.

"Wait for what! Maya is the cause for all this destruction. It's time she's held accountable once and for all."

"It's not that simple. There's a lot at stake here."

"Yeah, like Aaliyah's life. We have to find out if Aaliyah is dead or alive. Maya would know."

"Aaliyah is alive."

"We don't know that," Amir snapped angrily.

"Yes, we do. She called Precious a few days ago. The same day Skylar was taken."

"What Aaliyah say?"

"That she would be home in a week. Precious believes that. So do I and so does Nico. We have to be very strategic with Maya. We don't know what her and Arnez have planned. If she knows we're on to her, there's no telling what she might do."

"You're talking about Skylar right now aren't you?"

"Maya wasn't even on my radar an hour ago, but after speaking to you about how you met Latreese, it has to be somebody on the inside helping Arnez pull this off. Or maybe Maya is actually pulling the strings, but wants it to appear that Arnez is behind everything. I'm not sure, but

I don't want us to make a move until we're sure." Genesis was adamant about that. If Maya was the one responsible for Skylar's kidnapping, he knew he had to play his cards carefully, if there was any chance of Genesis getting her back alive.

Chapter Twenty-One

Forgiveness

"Precious, I was thrilled when Daddy said you wanted us to meet for dinner." Maya grinned at Quentin and then back at Precious.

"I wanted to personally apologize to you, Maya. I was wrong. I know now that you aren't responsible for Aaliyah's disappearance. I let our past issues get the best of me and I'm sorry."

"I'm so proud of you, Precious, for being able to admit you're wrong," Quentin said squeezing

Precious' hand.

"I have to admit, I'm very surprised by your sudden change. What brought that on?" Maya questioned, playing with the straw in her drink. Maya made no attempt to hide her skepticism.

"Because we found out who is behind everything."

"Precious, you didn't tell me that," Quentin said taken aback by the unexpected news.

"I only got confirmation late last night. That's what prompted me to call you this morning to see if Maya was available for dinner."

"I see. So who is it... who is this person? Father, wouldn't you like to know?" Maya asked staring at Quentin.

"Of course I want to know. This person has turned our lives upside down. I want to know who the lowlife scum is."

"I've already said too much. We're still searching for the person so we're keeping things very guarded until we can make our move," Precious revealed.

"We're not anybody, Precious. We're you're family. You can trust us." Quentin sounded offended that his daughter wouldn't open up to them.

"Daddy is right. If you're serious about building a relationship then I think we should all be honest with each other."

Precious glanced at her father and Maya. She put her head down as if she was battling herself about what she should do.

"Quentin, please don't mention this to anyone, especially Genesis and Nico."

"You have my word."

Precious then turned her attention to Maya. "Can I count on you to keep this to yourself?"

"Of course. I don't want to do anything to jeopardize our relationship, Precious."

"It's a man named Gomez Vargas. He's the one responsible for this."

"Wasn't his name in those reports that we read from the private investigator?" Quentin stated.

"Yes. Genesis was able to dig deeper and he is positive that this Vargas guy is the one who took Aaliyah. Not only that, shot at you Quentin, attacked our warehouse causing me to get shot and lose my memory and even kidnapped Genesis's girlfriend, Skylar."

"Wow, that's crazy. Where is this Vargas person?" Maya inquired.

"That's the million dollar question. Genesis has been to his lounge looking for him and he has several men on it. There was a sighting of him in Washington Heights, but by the time Genesis and his people got there, Vargas was gone."

"That's unfortunate. I wish I could do something to help," Maya said with concern.

"We're not giving up. Genesis is determined to find him... we all are."

Good luck with that, Precious. You all have looked everywhere but the one place you might find Gomez Vargas... the morgue. Hmmm, I wonder how long you dumbasses will be chasing a dead man who has absolutely nothing to do with all your despair. Tsk... Tsk... Tsk... So much precious time... Ha! The play on words is hilarious... is being wasted searching for the wrong man. Sister dear, your enemy is sitting right across from you, Maya thought to herself, disguising her devilish smile with a sweet, innocent grin.

"Just know, we're here for you. I always said Aaliyah was coming home and my faith in that has not wavered." Quentin reached over and hugged Precious.

"He's right, Precious. We are here for you." Maya got up from her chair and walked over to join in for a group hug. We're family and family sticks together."

After her dinner with Precious and Quentin, Maya had one other stop to make before heading home. She arrived at the hotel on Madison Avenue right before eleven. She was over an hour late, but Maya's dinner with her father and sister was much more important to her. She already had a key so she took the elevator to the twenty-fifth floor and let herself in.

"You were supposed to be here over an hour ago," Emory said when Maya entered the living room area of his hotel suite.

"I know, but I couldn't get out of this dinner with my father and sister," Maya said, kissing Emory on the back of his neck. She loved how sexy and masculine he was. Although Emory was younger than Maya, he always tried to act like he ran her which she got a kick out of.

"Do you think spending that much time with the two of them together is wise? You better hope they're not on to you."

"Trust me, they're not. My poor father is oblivious to anything when it comes to me and he's actually convinced Precious to give me another chance. Talk about dumb and dumber." Maya laughed, pouring herself some champagne that was on the table.

"I hope you know what you're doing because we might have a problem."

"What the fuck is wrong now?" Maya sighed.

"Arnez. The other day when we were meeting at the warehouse, Supreme paid him a visit."

"Get the hell out of here! You're just now telling me this shit!" Maya screamed.

"Calm yo' ass down before somebody calls hotel security on us," Emory cracked. "I've been dealing with my brother. He stressing over Aaliyah and shit. I'm stressing about Arnez. Then I'm wondering why in the fuck, this meeting we was supposed to have with a new connect hasn't gone down yet. So excuse me, if telling you about Supreme's visit wasn't at the top of my list."

"Just tell me what Supreme wanted."

"He told Arnez he believed he was responsible for Aaliyah being missing or knew who was."

"Are you serious?"

"Yes, and Arnez denied it of course, but Supreme let it be known that if Aaliyah didn't come home soon, there would be hell to pay starting with him."

"Did Arnez admit anything to you regarding Aaliyah?"

"Nope. He swore to me that he had nothing to do with her going missing. But my gut is telling me he's lying," Emory huffed. "Yo' if Arnez has anything to do with Aaliyah's disappearance I can't fuck wit' that dude and I told him that shit.

My brother loves that girl. He'll wanna kill my motherfuckin' ass if he think I have anything to do wit' her disappearance."

"Baby, relax. That's not gonna happen," Maya said stroking the back of Emory's head.

"I can't relax. Shit was going so smoothly and then Aaliyah has to come up missing. Arnez has me so pissed right now."

"In the heat of all your anger, you didn't mention to Arnez our involvement, did you?"

"Hell no! I ain't crazy. One of the reasons shit has been going so lovely is because you're able to keep tabs on Arnez and let me know what his next move is gonna be. That would all come to a halt if he found out we were working together and sleeping together too."

"I had to make sure. I know how you get when you're angry. We don't want to let our emotions ruin what we've worked so hard for."

"If what Supreme said is true, then Arnez is gonna be responsible for ruining our hard work."

"Let me handle Arnez. I'll talk to him and see if he has anything to do with Aaliyah's disappearance. If he does, then we'll decide what our next move should be."

"And what happened to the meeting with the new connect? You've cancelled twice. What's the hold up?"

"I don't know. I spoke to Gomez a few times and he's had to cancel. Now I can't get in touch with him at all. It's like he's vanished. Maybe he's gotten himself caught up in some bullshit. We might have to cut our losses with Gomez and find someone else," Maya suggested.

"Damn, ain't nothing going right."

"You're so tense. You need to relax, baby. All will be fine. Let me help you feel better." Maya gave Emory a seductive smile as she got down on her knees. She unzipped his jeans, pulled down his underwear and began sprinkling soft kisses on the tip of his hardened dick. Emory closed his eyes and leaned his head back relishing in the softness of Maya's lips. Maya opened wide deep throating him as Emory got lost in the wetness of her mouth.

Chapter Twenty-Two

Rescue Me

Genesis was on his way out the door when his phone started ringing. He hesitated for a moment, but then answered the call.

"Hello."

"How are you, Genesis? It's been a very long time." Genesis instantly recognized the voice on the phone.

"Arnez... you've finally decided to come out of hiding. I was beginning to think that rumors of you being alive were greatly exaggerated."

"I had to wait for the perfect time to make my presence known. That time has come."

"You've gone through a lot of trouble to cause the people in my life grief. Is this call to further antagonize me by letting me know you're not done yet?"

"Quite the opposite." Arnez chuckled. "This call is to try and make amends. I've taken so much from you. It's only right that I give something back."

"Arnez, stop talking in circles and get to the point 'cause I don't have time for this bullshit."

"What's the rush? Two former rivals catching up on old times. I'm enjoying myself."

"You'll be enjoying yourself without me. Now that I know for a fact I'm not chasing a ghost, I will hunt you down and I will kill you. Until then, we have nothing else to discuss."

"Don't hang up!" Arnez yelled out, right when Genesis was about to press end on his phone. "I have something to tell you that I know you want to hear."

"Then say it now or I'm hanging up," Genesis warned.

"You take all the fun away."

"Bye, Arnez."

"Okay, you win. As I was saying, I've taken so

much from you; I want to give something back. I'll even let you decide what it will be."

"You're still talking in riddles."

"Then let me get right to the point. If you had a choice to either save your old love, Talisa, or your new love, Skylar, who would you choose?"

"What type of question is that... Talisa is dead. You killed her on our wedding day... remember."

"That's the strange thing about death, you're never really sure. I'm the perfect example of that," Arnez boasted. "Now to be fair, I'm going to give you some time to consider your options. After all this time, you can very well be over your dead wife and mother of your child. If so, then it would only make sense to save the life of your new love. I've taken two women that you love away from you. I'm willing to return one. You decide who that will be. I'll be in touch."

It was Genesis' turn to scream out for Arnez not to hang up, but he was gone. He had delivered the cryptic message he wanted Genesis to receive. Now the games could truly begin.

"Where am I!" Skylar cried out when she woke

up. She realized she was lying in the center of a beautiful white canopy bed. The windows were open and a warm gust of wind was blowing the silk chiffon curtains. If Skylar hadn't remembered she was snatched off the streets of New York City, knocked out, woke up on a private plane and then knocked out again, she would've sworn she had retreated to an exotic island.

Skylar got out the bed and saw she was wearing the same clothes from the day she was kidnapped. She walked towards the open doors. It led to a beach that had the whitest sand she had ever seen. Then Skylar saw a woman. Her hair was in two French braids that reached her waist. It was as if a pair of scissors had never touched a strand of her hair. The closer she came it seemed as if her skin was glimmering. Her beauty was completely natural, like she only fed her body the healthiest food and drenched it with the purest water.

"Where am I?" Skylar asked the woman when she reached the door.

"I don't know. I thought you would be able to tell me."

"I have no clue, but it's beautiful here," Skylar said looking all around.

"Yes, it is. It would be paradise if guards didn't surround it. We're prisoners."

"How long have you been here?"

"I've lost track of time, but many, many years. But I haven't given up hope. I still believe that one day I'll be able to go home to my husband and child."

"You're married... does your husband know you're alive?" Skylar wanted to know, intrigued by this island beauty.

"No, he believes I'm dead. In many ways I am. But one day he'll come for me."

"Who... your husband?"

"Yes. He has to."

"I want you to be right. I have a child and a wonderful man that I want to get back home to."

"You will." The woman stroked the side of Skylar's arm. Her spirit was warm and gentle.

"Thank you. You have such a beautiful aura. I'm sorry. I'm asking you all these questions, but I haven't even told you my name. I'm Skylar," she said reaching out her hand.

"Nice to meet you, Skylar. I haven't had any companions since I've been here. The only people I talk to are the ones who take care of me. I know you don't want to be here, but I appreciate the company."

"I can only imagine. I have so many more questions I want to ask you. Like how did you end up here, who brought you here? But before

I flood you with questions, what's your name?"

"Talisa. My name is Talisa."

"Precious, come in." Quentin beamed, happy to see his daughter. "First dinner yesterday, now you're stopping by to visit me. What have I done to deserve all this special attention from my daughter?"

"This isn't exactly a social visit, Quentin."

"Then what is it about? Did you find something out about Aaliyah... is she okay?"

"Do you really want to know the answer to that?"

"What kind of question is that, Precious? You know I would do anything for my granddaughter."

"I'm glad you said that because there is something I need you to do for Aaliyah."

"Tell me. Whatever it is, I'll do it."

"Do you know if Maya is home right now?"

"I spoke to her a few minutes ago and she was home, why?"

"After I leave here, I'm going to Maya's place. I need for you to call her and tell her that we believe we've found Aaliyah's location and we might be able to bring her home as soon as tomorrow."

"Is that true? That's great news!"

"No, it's not true, Quentin."

"What the hell are you up to, Precious?"

"Getting to the truth."

"I can't believe you," Quentin flung his arms up. "All that crap you said at the dinner table last night was lies? You still believe Maya is responsible?"

"Yes, I do. And if you think she's innocent then you'll do what I asked."

"How is me calling Maya with a bunch of lies going to prove anything?"

"Because if Maya is guilty, when she gets off the phone with you, she's heading straight to wherever Aaliyah is being held, to kill her."

"You don't even know if Aaliyah is being held in New York," Quentin said angrily.

"There's only one way to find out, isn't there. If Maya is as innocent as you seem to believe, after you make the phone call, she'll keep her ass right there in the house. But now that her guard is down and she no longer thinks I feel she's the enemy, Maya will go finish Aaliyah off. She has no choice."

"Why would you say that?"

"Because Aaliyah can identify Maya as her

kidnapper, that's why. She can't allow Aaliyah to expose the web of lies she weaved."

"I don't want any part of this!" Quentin roared. "You refuse to let go of this vendetta you have against your sister."

"And you refuse to see the truth. What are you so afraid of! To have to acknowledge your daughter is a monster? Do you not understand what she's done? Amir's girlfriend Latreese, her real name is Kendra Watkins. She was a prostitute hired by Maya to target Amir. Why? So she could get inside information to what was going on within our organization. We believe Maya is the one that killed Latreese too. She might have even helped Arnez take Skylar. That's only the recent stuff. Let's not even go back to all the other tragedies she's responsible for."

"I can't hear anymore of this," Quentin said, wanting to silence Precious.

"You will stand here and you will listen to me!" Precious had fire in her eyes and she was not backing down. "If you love your granddaughter as much as you claim then you will do this. If my daughter dies because you rather embrace a lie than face the truth, not only will I kill Maya... I'm coming for you."

Quentin broke down and fell back on his favorite recliner chair. Whenever he had a problem or was overcome with sadness, this was the chair he turned to. It gave Quentin comfort and peace. It also seemed to bring about clarity to any issue he was struggling with.

"I'll make the call. But after this, I'm done with you and this hatred you have for your sister. If you don't let it go, it will eat you alive and destroy everyone you love."

"Quentin, I honestly feel sorry for you. You're not faking it. Maya has you so wrapped that you can't even think rationally when it comes to her." Precious paused for a moment, tempted to shed a tear for her father, but now wasn't the time. She needed to save her tears for Aaliyah. "Make the phone call and then pray. I'll also be praying for you. Because when you can no longer deny the truth about Maya, I'm afraid you might die of a broken heart."

Maya was getting dolled up before she went to meet Emory at his hotel. She wanted to wear something sexy and enticing. So she pulled out one of her favorite dresses. It was a cutout silk maxi with ethereal paisley print, rivet trim around the neck, cuffs, waist and back. It had long blouson sleeves, keyhole front, cutout waist, back and a pleated skirt. Maya completed her look with a bun and light make-up. She twirled around in front of her floor length mirror admiring her attire.

"Emory, you will not be able to keep your hands off of me when I arrive wearing this," Maya said blowing herself a kiss in the mirror. She sprayed a little bit more perfume and was ready to be on her way. "That must be Emory," Maya said reaching for her phone.

She glanced down at the number and saw that is was her father. Maya debated taking the call, as she was anxious to get to Emory. He was amazing in bed, much better than Arnez. "It could be important," Maya said answering the call. "Hi, Daddy what's going on?"

"Precious just called me with some good news and I wanted to share it with you."

"What kind of good news?" Maya asked trying to sound like she cared although she could give a flying fuck.

"Supreme believes he's located Aaliyah."

"Really? That's great. So where is she?"

"She was excited and rushing me off the phone so I didn't get a lot of details. All she said was, Supreme has a great lead on Aaliyah's location and by tomorrow he would be bringing her home."

"That really is great news, Daddy. So Supreme hasn't actually found Aaliyah yet," Maya wanted to confirm.

"No, not yet, but he's very close. Precious is ecstatic and so am I."

"Me too, Daddy. Thanks so much for calling and letting me know."

"Maya, before you go."

"Yes."

"I haven't eaten dinner yet. Why don't we meet for dinner at that restaurant you love so much."

"Gosh, Dad, that sounds great, but I've already got plans and I can't cancel."

"Come on, Maya. I really want you to meet me for dinner," Quentin pleaded.

"Daddy, I can't," Maya replied firmly. "Tomorrow... we can have dinner tomorrow. My treat. I have to go, Daddy. I love you."

Maya ended the call furious about what her father told her. "I blame you for this Arnez," she screamed, grabbing her purse and car keys before hurrying out. Once Maya was in the car she called Emory.

"Are you on the way?" Emory asked when he answered.

"No, there's been a change of plans."

"Why, what's going on?"

"I had an opportunity to speak to Arnez. You were right."

"He has Aaliyah... where is she?"

"She's dead." There was an unnerving silence. "Emory, are you there?"

"I'm here. Arnez killed Aaliyah?"

"Yes, but he claimed it was an accident. He said he caught her snooping around the warehouse in Staten Island. There was a struggle, she bumped her head and died."

"That fuckin' bastard. What am I going to tell my brother?" Emory mumbled sounding like he was in shock.

"Don't tell him anything. It's time for you to get rid of Arnez. He is bringing way too much heat our way. Once Supreme realizes his precious daughter is dead, all hell is gonna break loose. You need to kill Arnez tonight," Maya insisted.

"I agree. I'ma call him now and tell him we need to meet."

"Don't give him any indication that you know he murdered Aaliyah. Play it cool."

"I know how to handle Arnez."

"Okay, just be careful. Arnez is no dummy. Call me when it's done. I'll meet you at your hotel later on."

"That works. I'll be in touch," Emory said

ending the call. Maya was keeping her finger crossed that he didn't fuck things up because Arnez was not someone you underestimated. Maya's thoughts switched from Emory and Arnez to Aaliyah.

"Your time is finally up, Aaliyah. There won't be an Arnez to the rescue. It's lights out." Maya giggled tossing her phone over to the passenger seat. "Ready or not here I come." She pressed down on the gas, eager to be rid of Aaliyah once and for all.

Precious was on Maya's ass making sure not to let her out of sight. She kept enough distance between the cars not to alert Maya that she was being followed.

After all these years of constantly getting a pass for your destructive behavior, that ends tonight. You're going down Maya and not even Quentin can be your savior. Just take me to my daughter so I can do what I should've done a long time ago... kill you, Precious was shaken out of her thoughts when she saw Xavier was calling her.

"Hey, Xavier. Are you getting a little lonely being home alone?" Precious joked as she made a quick right turn, making sure to keep up with

Maya.

"I'm not alone. Grandfather is here. He's worried. Where are you?"

"I don't know the exact location. Somewhere in Brooklyn."

"Are you following Maya?"

"Is that what your grandfather told you?"

"Hold on, Mom. He wants to speak to you." Xavier handed his grandfather the phone.

"Precious, I don't have a good feeling about this. I want you to stop following Maya and come home."

"So she can kill my daughter? Are you crazy!"

"I'll handle Maya."

"Now you want to handle Maya. So are you saying you believe me now?"

"What I'm saying is, I don't see anything good coming from this. I'm about to call Maya and tell..."

"Don't you dare!" Precious barked, cutting Quentin off. "You let me handle this. I'm sick of you always getting involved and saving Maya's treacherous ass. Maybe if you would've stepped up a long time ago, Aaliyah wouldn't be in the predicament she is in now. I have to go and Quentin, stay out of it."

Precious got off the phone with Quentin just in time because Maya had parked and was getting out her car. Precious slowed down and turned left on the first street she came to so Maya couldn't see her. She parked on one of the side streets trying to be as discreet as possible.

"Let me take both my guns so I'll have extra protection in case something goes wrong," Precious said, talking to herself out loud. She reached inside the hidden compartment making sure to have a weapon in the front and the back.

Precious sprinted across the street wanting to walk on the side with no lights. She stood back behind a tree when she saw a figure cut across the yard. She couldn't tell if it was Maya or not. A few seconds later, Precious saw the figure again go up some stairs and turn the corner. This time she was almost sure it was Maya so she dashed in that direction with caution. When Precious got up the stairs and turned the corner she had no idea if Maya went up the other flight of stairs or if she went down.

Fuck! Where the hell did she go! Precious shouted to herself. Precious decided to take the stairs going down. The moment her Timberland boot touched the step, Precious felt the tip of a gun on the side of her head.

"Move!" Maya roared then snatched the gun Precious was holding out of her hand. "When Quentin wouldn't stop blowing up my phone,

I knew something was up. Then I peeped you tryna sneak up on me like a snake. Don't make me blow your brains out right here on these stairs, so keep it cute," Maya advised, shoving Precious inside the apartment.

"Arnez, is that you," Precious could hear Aaliyah call out.

"No, baby, it's me."

"Mom!" Aaliyah came running over to Precious squeezing her tightly. "I can't believe you're here. I missed you so much," Aaliyah wept.

"I missed you too, baby," Precious cried, holding on to Aaliyah just as tight.

"Okay... okay... I'll give the two of you a few minutes to do all that hugging and kissing," Maya snickered.

"Mom, what are you doing here?" Aaliyah questioned, ignoring Maya's taunting.

"I can answer that," Maya jumped in and said without giving Precious a chance to respond. "Your mother has this terrible habit of always wanting to play hero. It never gets her anywhere. But on a positive note, at least mother and daughter will die together."

"Yo' this heifa is so fuckin' crazy!" Aaliyah uttered.

"Calm down." Precious patted her daughter's hand, not wanting Aaliyah to get worked up.

"Yes, calm your little mutt down. Some pets aren't worth keeping around. That would be you, Aaliyah, in case you weren't able to follow what I was saying." Maya laughed.

"I'm glad you think this is funny, Maya."

"Oh, stop being so serious, Precious. If you would've stayed home like a good little wife.... wait... are you still married. I can't keep up, but anywho. If you would've minded your business I wouldn't have to kill you. I mean I kinda like you, Precious. You're my sister. Your daughter, on the other hand, I was looking forward to watching her die."

"You don't want to do this, Maya. Quentin will know you killed us. He'll never forgive you. He has been the only person that is always on your side. Do you want him to turn his back on you too?"

"I'm not worried about our father. I'll come up with a story and he'll so desperately want to believe it that he'll convince himself that it's true. The only people who can dispute it will be dead."

"I guess you forgot about Arnez. He's never gonna let my father, Supreme, think that he killed us. He will turn on you so fast."

"You're absolutely right," Maya hummed. "That's why Arnez is dead or being killed as we speak."

"You really ain't loyal to nobody," Aaliyah scoffed.

"Yes, I am. I'm loyal to myself. Speaking of which, I have a date. Don't I look fabulous in this dress." Maya did a quick pose. "I'm getting off track. Yeah, I have a date so we need to get this over with. Who wants to die first?"

Precious and Aaliyah gave Maya a blank stare. Her level of crazy was beyond their comprehension. They eyed each other as if asking was Maya serious with her antics.

"Sooooo… who wants to die first? Can you all discuss this quickly because like I said, I do have a date tonight."

"Can we have a moment?" Precious asked Maya.

"I suppose, but make it quick."

Precious moved a couple feet over for a little privacy to speak to Aaliyah. "Look at me," Precious said lifting Aaliyah's chin. "I love you and your brother more than anything in this world. No matter what happens, you make sure you always look out for Xavier. I want you to take care of Supreme and Nico too. They're going to need you so you have to be strong for them. I know they act tough, but they're both so sweet and vulnerable. Will you do that for me?"

"Mom, please stop." Aaliyah's eyes watered

up.

"Don't you dare cry. You hear me. We will not give Maya the satisfaction of watching us cry."

"Can you all hurry this up! I don't have all night. Say your mushy goodbyes so we can get this show over with," Maya grunted.

"We're almost done. Just a couple more minutes," Precious said. "Now listen to me very carefully. When I tell you to run you run and don't stop running until you're out of harm's way and you're able to get some help. Do you understand?"

"Mom, what are you gonna do?"

"Get you out of here alive."

"Either we're both getting out of here alive or we will both die here together and I mean that," Aaliyah stated not backing down. "Don't try to change my mind 'cause it ain't gonna happen."

"Why the hell do you have to be so damn stubborn." Precious shook her head.

"I get it from my mama." Aaliyah smiled. "Are you ready to do this?"

"Always." Precious grabbed her daughter and held her as if it might be the very last time. "I love you, Aaliyah."

"I love you, too."

Without saying another word, Aaliyah reached in the back of her mother's jeans and retrieved her gun. She spun Precious around to make sure she didn't get shot in the crossfire. Aaliyah and Maya both blasted simultaneously and all anyone heard was the echo of bullets being discharged.

"Noooooo!" Precious wailed as she lunged at Maya with all her strength. With the nonstop tugging of the trigger, bullets were flying everywhere and no one knew who would live or who would die.